GW00503604

For the nourishers of the world and its people. And especially, for those who have nourished me.

LET ME BEGIN AGAIN

Caroline Bond

Somer

One

It was a perfect day to go hiking. The skies were blue and the air was crisp. Leaves were beginning to become brilliant reds and yellows. It was not a terribly difficult hike for them, and any difficulty was worth the beauty all around them. It was a hike Sydney loved but Natalie had never been on. After half an hour they forked away from a well-worn trail and walked through the dense brush. After another half an hour they reached a vast rock structure. The rocks peaked at a cliff, and the edge dropped to a creek below.

Natalie and Sydney stood at the brink of the cliff and looked down at the shallow water, marveling at the way that nature held them on all sides. They sat on the edge of the cliff with their legs hanging off and Natalie pointed out Sydney's untied shoe. Even though Sydney loved being up there it also made her nervous to be at the precipice of a free fall. She said she would wait until they got up to leave to tie her shoe, not wanting to lean over the edge of the cliff. Seconds later Sydney hastily jumped up as though she were suddenly spooked.

Sydney turned around on the ball of her foot and took a step. Sydney did not realize when she jumped up she had stepped on her right shoelace with her left foot. As soon as she lifted her leg to step forward she was caught by the shoelace.

Had it been anywhere else Sydney would have fallen, perhaps hitting her side or breaking the fall with her arm, she might have even been hurt. She would have laughed at her clumsiness. This time was different though. In Sydney's eagerness to walk away from the cliff she too violently lifted her foot. She started to topple forward and then when correcting this she stepped backward but found nothing but air waiting for her foot. Natalie watched in horror as this happened both fast and slow, in an instant and an eternity. Sydney was face up as she plunged toward the creek below. Her blond, curly hair looked wild and loose. Her face was paralyzed. Sydney's long legs were slightly bent. She wore shorts and her legs looked vulnerable. Natalie thought they made eye contact but Sydney's eyes fluttered everywhere, looking at nothing. Sydney's head and back both hit rocks.

In a panic Natalie ran around to the bottom. She was more frightened than she had ever been. "Please God," she pleaded over and over. She almost tripped several times in her haste. When she was near the bottom her steps became more reckless and she did trip. Natalie fell on outstretched hands but unlike Sydney, she was unhurt. Total, it took an agonizing three minutes to reach Sydney, and when she did, she wished she hadn't. Sydney was dead. As soon as Natalie saw her, she knew this. Natalie felt for a pulse and listened for breathing, but she knew there would be none. Still, she mustered up all the knowledge she had from a CPR class she had taken in college, and pumped and breathed and pumped and breathed and pumped and breathed until she collapsed. Nothing. The water was tinged red with blood. Sydney looked calm, she was gone. There was no life in her face.

"No," Natalie yelled, "Please God, no!" Sydney's eyes were wide open and Natalie was overcome with terror. She felt paralyzed, but knew the only thing she could do was leave Sydney there, alone, and find someone to help. She pushed her dark brown hair out of her face. She was clammy and close to hyperventilating.

All her memories of Sydney quickly infiltrated Natalie's mind. They had worked together at the bank. They were both tellers, both seeing it as a holding position, not what they wanted to do long-term. They sat next to each other and had connected instantly.

Natalie and Sydney's friendship was compartmentalized, not really reaching outside of work until this day they went hiking. It had been a long time coming, extending their friendship outside of work, and neither of them were sure of why it hadn't happened already. Sydney was outgoing and fun, often joking around at work, but a very conscientious worker. Sydney was a person who was just simply, free. Natalie appreciated this about Sydney but was herself a much more serious and intense person. Despite this, she was less conscientious, often slipping into a daydream.

Sydney had gone away to college but come back to her hometown of Carlton, North Carolina. Sydney had wanted to be near her family in Carlton. While she was fun-loving, she also took her relationships seriously, and had missed her parents and brother and sister when she had gone to college.

Natalie had come to Carlton for college and hadn't left. Carlton was a small town, but it seemed to fit Natalie's more serious personality. Natalie had gone to Vance College. There wasn't a lot of partying or loudness there. Carlton was quaint, and Vance was tiny. Its small, close-knit community was comforting to Natalie.

After this rundown went through her mind, which had stalled her for only a few moments, Natalie closed Sydney's eyes and turned to go back up to the top of the cliff. When she reached the top she began to run in the direction they had come.

Natalie's intention was to run toward someone who could help. That was not an intention that was filled. In Natalie's panic as well as unfamiliarity with the route, she did not go back the way they had come. Before long she realized she had no sense of where she was or how to get back. Natalie stood still, not knowing what to do or which way to go. She tried to backtrack to a place that looked familiar but only became more hopelessly lost.

A bird came then, a small, round, speckled bird. It perched on Natalie's shoulder, stepping on her hair. It was as though it were looking out at the world with her, its personality too, seemed quiet and serious. The bird then flew in front of her face, looking her in the eyes. She was grateful for the companionship and was centered, for just a moment. The bird flew up in the air and away. Not knowing what else to do she followed the bird, dodging the brush and trees. She thought of nothing but the breathless sensation of running. Natalie's breathing was slightly labored when after five minutes, the bird finally landed on a tree stump in a clearing. Natalie sat on the stump next to the little creature. The stump looked like it had been cut down many years before.

As Natalie looked down at the stump's worn surface she saw something she had not noticed at first. There was a square outline on the stump with a rough looking handle on one side and two hinges on the other. It looked like a door, but surely it wasn't a door. That didn't make any sense. Gingerly, she grasped the handle and pulled up. It was a door, it opened, and she saw that there were steps leading down into darkness. Natalie could not will herself to leave, nor to take the first step down into the darkness. She wanted to turn around and run, to somehow make it to the parking lot. She stood at the edge of the stairs for long and drawn out minutes, in the same nervous way she had stood at the edge of the cliff.

Natalie listened to the sounds of the forest. She listened to her breath, changing from coarse to silent. She was lost in both the thought of the choice that lay in front of her, to go down the steps or leave, and her curiosity of where the steps led. Sometime during these moments the bird must have flown away. Natalie twisted and turned, suddenly remembering it, looking all around, but it was not in her view.

Now Natalie stood, bird-less, in an unknown part of the forest, and her sense of urgency came back. Sydney's accident exploded into her consciousness, along with the magnitude of Sydney's death. Natalie became desperate for escape, for the thoughts of Sydney's death to be chased out of her mind. Her need for postponement of reality laid a path of courageousness. She stepped onto the top step and then descended into the darkness. The stairwell had roots on either side, twisted and old. She touched the cold shell of one of the roots with her fingertips. She shuddered, from the drop in temperature and from her apprehension and fear. She took each step with care, slowly descending into the cool, dark air. Her eyes, as she stepped down, looked only at the steps, of which there were five. There was a light on at the bottom and with each successive step, the outline of the stairs became more visible. She put her foot onto the dirt floor after the last step with a hesitancy that had heightened during the slow descent. At the bottom she stood in a dim room, a cove really. She stood firmly physically but did not feel at all grounded. The room was the size of a large closet, one that would fit all her clothes and her excessive pairs of shoes. The floor, walls, and ceiling were all dirt and a light bulb hung from the ceiling. It barely illuminated the room.

In front of her was a slide projector. She had not seen one of those in years. She wondered if she was hallucinating. She was certain it had not been there just a moment before. Natalie touched the projector lightly and it seemed that it really was there. She turned it on, not expecting it to work, but it did. Shining on the dirt wall was a picture of her mom, young and clearly pregnant, her dad, herself, and a baby, who must have been her brother. She flipped to the next slide. She was filled with a new image. She and her mom were in the same location and wearing the same clothes as in the previous slide. She was touching her mom's belly. She flipped to the next slide. The next picture was in a hospital room. Her dad sat on the edge of the bed and she sat on his lap. Her mom was holding a tiny baby. Her brother sat on her mom's legs and was touching the baby on the cheek. Natalie remembered that day and she remembered her baby sister, Somer, but she had never seen this picture.

Two

Somer was born when Natalie was four. Natalie was the oldest, and she had watched her mom's belly grow in anticipation of a little sister. She marveled at the way her sister was inside her mom. She made plans to be the big sister to the new baby; she would babysit, give her bottles, read to her, snuggle with her, and be her overall protector. Sure, she had a brother, but a sister would be a miniature version of herself and her mom, she thought. Somer came, red with a slightly bluish tint. Natalie was not there for the actual birth but was whisked in later with her brother. Tiny Somer did not breathe well from the beginning. She was put in an incubator and had many tubes attached to her as her breathing and heart became weaker. This scared Natalie, who so desperately wanted to protect her. Somer looked just as Natalie had looked as a baby. She had dark hair and delicate features. Despite the incubator and tubes that seemed to grow out of her, Somer did not live through the day. Natalie's memories of that day were one big, foggy, overwhelming picture. When she thought of it, and now, looking at the picture, her head swam and her thoughts circled in a blur. It had been traumatic, losing her sister so completely. She had never gotten the chance to know her, and she had certainly failed to protect her.

On second glance Natalie saw pain that lay beneath the happy exterior in the picture of them all in the hospital. This was before Somer's body had begun to rapidly decline and perhaps none of them had known that she would soon be in a tiny casket and buried, unable to be touched. They knew something was wrong from the beginning though. It happened fast, and Natalie had not completely known what happened. She did not comprehend what the closed casket meant. She just knew that Somer had been there, and then she had become sick, and then she was gone. Somer's death not been explained to young Natalie.

The funeral was quick and private and part of the haze of memories from Somer's life. It was a cloudy day, but the weather had been nice. Somer had been born in the fall, when everything was starting to die; it seemed cruel to Natalie that

Somer was included in this fate. Natalie was there with her parents, her brother, and grandparents. Even aunts and uncles hadn't been invited. They followed the hearse in their car, her father driving. Natalie remembered looking directly out the window, looking at everything, not understanding that the car in front of them carried her dead sister. Even as she put the flower on her sister's casket while she held her grandmother's hand, she did not know what was going on until she looked back on that day much later.

There was not really any ceremony. A great deal of ceremony, Natalie thought now, would have been too much acknowledgement. Acknowledgement was repeatedly discouraged, not just then, but for Natalie's whole life. After the funeral came and went, a slow trickle of people came to their house. Her mother slammed the door in their faces when they brought food. "I'll never be hungry again," she told them. Natalie stood at her mother's side a couple of times when this happened, and remembered the anger in her voice. When her father answered the door he would gently explain the food away, thanking them for the thought, but saying it was too painful for his wife to have any more acknowledgement of their loss. "Give the food to someone who needs it," he would tell them. This milder approach did not stand out in her memory as much, but still, she remembered the sad gentleness in his voice.

Cards that even suggested sympathy were sent back unopened. Natalie remembered her mother letting out a desperate cry each day when the mail came. "Get rid of these, send them back," she would say to her Natalie's father. It was understood by all close to the family it was a subject not to be talked about. This was never explicitly told to Natalie, but she always knew. It was a subject that soon became a non-subject. Somer's death was presumably rarely thought about and not widely known. Natalie almost convinced herself it was a bad dream, but it was not, and the loss of her sister was always with her. What she never knew was that though the memories were fleeting to her, it was something that was, in fact, thought about by her mother and father constantly.

When Natalie was nine, she discovered a picture from the day Somer was born. Natalie was looking for her gymnastics camp t-shirt, and was hoping it had gotten stuck in her mom's dresser. The picture was in her mom's bottom drawer. Natalie had not known the picture of Natalie's mom and Somer were there, and she doubted her dad knew either. As shown from the beginning, Natalie's mom did not understand that her husband's pain was just as deep as her pain was. He too understood it as more her loss than his. Whether this understanding was accurate or not was lost in the truth that Natalie's mother did not cope with it as well as Natalie's father did. At least that's what it seemed like when you compared the crying spells with the stoicism. Natalie's mother, father, brother, nor herself came out of the loss unmarked.

Upon her death Somer went to live in the Holding Place. That is where she grew up. Like all those in in the Holding Place, she was given a task. It was a known task; unlike the way those who live on Earth often do not know what their task is (even though they all have one). Some on Earth do not realize it until they are very old, and some never do. On Earth there is so much else they contend with. Those who live in the Holding Place know from the start, they are assigned a task in an intentional, understandable way.

Somer's task was to spread joy. She felt like the luckiest girl in the Holding Place. Spreading joy was as much a gift to her as to others. Even more of a gift, she often thought. Joy seemed to come back to her triple-fold. Because she had died so young her task was more unstructured than those who came to the Holding Place as adults. Like a child may naturally bubble with joy, Somer learned how to hone hers, infect specific people in the Holding Place who needed it. Also because she had been so young, her task did not involve people on Earth. She needed more protected experiences in those formative years as she grew into a young woman.

Somer lived with her expanded family. She had parents, siblings, cousins, aunts, uncles, and grandparents. Some of this family had ties or common bloodlines on Earth, but not all. They came from many different backgrounds.

Where Somer grew up there was no disease and no brokenness. There was sadness, because sadness is authentic, and adds a layer of richness and realness to existence. Sadness was the conduit through which Somer got her greatest joy, infecting those who needed it with joy.

Somer always knew that the Holding Place was temporary, but she loved it. Each person in the Holding Place understood that it was temporary, just like Earth was. Some came and went in the same day. But some, who had completed their journey on Earth, were there for good. For those people, the Holding Place was also the Final Place. Those in the Holding Place, like those on Earth, were given to each other, to serve each other. Those in the Holding Place were not distracted by the world that surrounded those on Earth. They were not inundated with sorrow or trouble; they only had enough to keep them compassionate. They could focus on their tasks, and each other. There was a sense of wonder at the way everything that seemed unconnected on Earth came together in the Holding Place. People who had not been connected on

Earth became dear friends and family. Knowledge gained on Earth sometimes proved critical in the Holding Place. A person who was a mother on Earth might be given the task to raise those who died young. A writer on Earth might be one of the ones to put out the great Holding Place publication, which cross-pollinated the vast space with information about each corner and bit.

For those for whom the Holding Place was the Final Place, they are people who have lived their lives enough times over that they are able to fully forgive themselves for their mistakes, love others without selfishness, give for the joy of it, and not dwell in sorrow. They no longer need the lessons of hardship.

The older a person is when they die, the less time they are likely to spend in the Holding Place. Generally, the culmination of years a person will live, including those on Earth and the Holding Place before their next life, is between eighty and one hundred and fifty years. Someone like Somer, who was an infant when she died, would spend a long stretch in the Holding Place. After that time, they go back to Earth. They become different people, with different lives, but they are always in the family they love. Not always the family they were born into in the previous life, but people are never truly separated from the ones they love.

In the Holding Place, Somer grew up in a big white house with a wraparound porch and a yard that was cut once a year. It was cut in the fall, when the flowers that peppered the land in a swarm of color died. Somer had her own bedroom that was painted and repainted many different times as she grew up and developed new favorite colors. In her room there were many doors. Each door led to someone who had died, but deeply loved her. Some, who were together on Earth, were congregated and living together again. Because people die at different times they have to be absorbed by love and comfort during their new birth into the Holding Place. That is why each person who dies has an expanded family.

The door to Somer's grandparents on her father's side was right beside her bed. When she was very young she would go and curl up between her grandparents, and for a while when she was six she spent every night with them. Her grandparents had Somer's father very late in life, and then had both died young. They had each come into the Holding Place shortly after Somer. Somer's grandparents helped raise her. Somer never lacked for love in the Holding Place, her expanded family was filled with a family that fit her perfectly.

Just as Somer's task was to spread joy, the couple that raised Somer had the task of raising and giving guidance to the young. They were in the Holding Place as their Final Place. They raised many children who had died young and even children who had died in the womb. Somer loved them very much, and they, her. Even so, she was aware she also had parents and a brother and sister on Earth. She loved them very much too and she sometimes went and visited them. As a young child she loved visiting, she would dribble an imaginary basketball around her brother, sit on her sister's desk at school, or study her parents as they interacted with each other. Though there were many people who loved her in the Holding Place, sometimes she longed to be around her Earth family.

When Somer visited Earth, easily crossing the barrier from the Holding Place to Earth, she was completely invisible. Those on Earth could not sense her, see her, hear her, or feel her. She was non-existent to them while there, and this was something she understood with deep sadness. Somer knew her Earth family loved her, but she wanted so much for them to know her. As she grew up and into her teenage years she accepted more and more that there was a wedge between her and her human family. This was a wedge that always existed between the living and the dead. It was natural, one that could not be helped. These two worlds were intimately connected, all who lived on Earth had lived in the Holding Place and would eventually go back to the Holding Place, and all who lived in the Holding Place had lived on Earth and most would go back to Earth. Somer tried to let it be enough that one day her family would come to the Holding Place and would meet her. Despite her life and happiness in the Holding Place, a part Somer sincerely wished she could live with her Earth family.

When Somer visited her family she sensed anguish on Earth, a struggle among humans that she was not familiar with. This anguish, this struggle, did not exist where she had grown up. Still though, for as long as she could remember, she longed for an authentic human life, one where when she was young, she could wake up in the morning and hug her parents and play with her brother and sister. One where people on Earth would see her, talk to her, and know her. She wanted a life where she could eat the food on Earth and swim in the pools. She wanted to leave footprints, to be seen.

While Somer wanted a relationship with all of her Earth family, she had especially desired one with her sister, Natalie, for as long as she had known she had a sister on Earth. There was something special about a big sister. She imagined sleepovers in the living room, braiding each other's hair, and being able to talk about absolutely anything. She wanted to hear Natalie say her name. Somer hung onto Natalie, knowing and seeing her, but not being known and seen herself.

Three

Somer loved her family on Earth without pause. She didn't understand why Earth had so much more pain than the Holding Place. She wondered why it wasn't perfect, every gene mutation, accident, and sorrow avoided. Surely if that were possible in the Holding Place it was possible on Earth. Earth was cluttered with all kinds of messiness though. Each person had the choice to love the Earth despite the sorrow, to see the ways it was beautiful through the muddle. It was easy to love the Holding Place; it wasn't always easy to love Earth.

That day at the cliff, Somer was there. She sat on the edge of the cliff, invisible, beside Natalie and Sydney. Somer realized what was happening at the same time as Natalie and Sydney. She watched Sydney fall with the same horror Natalie had. She watched Natalie run around to Sydney's body. She listened as Natalie pleaded to make what happened be untrue. She did not go with Natalie though, when Natalie ran through the brush, frantically, to get help. She remained sitting, in the same position, trying to absorb what had happened. She sat, looking at Sydney below. As the time passed she wondered what happened to Natalie. Finally, she went back to the sturdy white house in the Holding Place. She curled up on her bed, scared.

Somer drifted off to sleep and when she woke she saw a new door had appeared among the many other doors in her bedroom. Her favorite color was purple, which was the color of her walls. Somer painted the room herself, and had been thrilled at the sense of accomplishment she had afterwards.

Somer panicked. Who had died? Someone must have died, each door led to someone who died. Somer gripped the doorknob and turned it but did not push the door open. She considered going to get her parents or grandparents but was full of curiosity. She tapped on the door, hard enough for it to slowly swing open.

There Natalie sat, absorbed in a picture from the day Somer was born projected onto the wall of the small room. Natalie's head turned and she was startled. Somer looked familiar to her, but she could not quite place her. Somer and

Natalie looked at each other, both riveted. The space was so silent that when Natalie said, "Hi?" it sounded like a roar.

Somer was shocked. Natalie did not know where she was or what was going on. Somer could think of no logical conclusion other than Natalie had died.

"Natalie?" Somer questioned, knowing it was her, but being unable to comprehend what was happening. "Natalie," she stated, knowing that it was Natalie who did not know who she was, "I can't believe you can see me. I don't know how to convince you this is true, but I'm your sister." Natalie looked puzzled. "I'm Somer, your sister who died," she clarified.

Natalie's heart skipped a beat. Natalie saw now that Somer looked familiar because she was looking at a reflection of herself. Somer's hair was brown, long and unkempt. Her skin was clear and ivory. Her eyes were big and inquisitive. She looked younger than her twenty years. Something about her face looked mischievous. Perhaps it was the way her eyes lit up as she talked and the slightest smile, really just a look of pleasantness was on her face.

It had already been an incredulous day for Natalie, and this fact lent itself to Natalie halfway believing that this young woman was her sister. Under normal circumstances she would have found way after way to discount Somer's claim. Was it possible this was her sister, who had died as an infant twenty years ago?

"Somer?" Natalie paused and watched Somer's eyes widen. That was the first time Somer had ever heard Natalie say her name. "Somer," Natalie said again, "What's happening?"

Somer did not answer but questioned Natalie, "Natalie, how did you die?"

"Somer," Natalie said, the name unfamiliar in her mouth, "I haven't died. Sydney is the one who died."

"You must have died," Somer responded, "that's the only way you could be here."

"Somer, I haven't died. My friend Sydney died," Natalie repeated. She looked back into Somer's eyes, her resolve and certainty fading. If this was truly Somer, and Somer had died, what did that mean for her? "I don't think I died," Natalie stammered, "Sydney fell and I tried to backtrack but got lost. After that there was a small bird I followed. Then I ended up here. Then there was the projector. Then there was you." Natalie felt dizzy after speaking so many unbelievable things.

Natalie was overwhelmed with the situation with Somer to the point Sydney had slipped to the back of her mind. She needed to go get help, but she did not know what to do. Sydney was out there, alone, and Somer was right in front of her. Both people were important and finding help for Sydney and staying with Somer each felt like the right choice. Leaving Sydney like that, dead at the bottom of the ravine, seemed like the worst thing she could do to her. This young woman who claimed she was Somer was right in front of her though, all grown up. Natalie was drawn to Somer. Her spirit was electric and contagious, and Natalie did not want the precious moment they were in to disintegrate. Somer was very still, as if moving might shatter everything.

Natalie's mind was filled with confusion. To believe this young woman standing right in front of her was a girl who had been dead twenty years and her sister was far-fetched. It made not a bit of sense. It was not possible, was it? Sure, she believed there was a God and an afterlife. She thought she believed that at least, but that did not mean Somer was there from the afterlife. The impossibility this was her sister was something she was certain of, something she had to be certain of, it was the only thing that made sense. Something tugged at her though. Unless she was dreaming, this could not be true. Certainty and doubt alternated, coming and going quickly and absolutely.

Then she knew, she was dreaming. That had to be it. She wondered how to get out of the dream. Maybe Sydney was not dead. She pinched herself hard. Wasn't that what people did to wake up from a dream? Nothing happened except for a dull ache where she pinched herself. She forced her eyes open as wide as she could, as though that would force closed eyes of sleep to open, but nothing changed. She held her breath, thinking that would cause her to wake up, gasping for air, but all that happened was the great need to get air into her lungs right where she was. Nothing was working, but that didn't convince her she wasn't dreaming. A dream made more sense than anything else that was happening and a new certainty surged.

If she was dreaming and with a sister who was a figment of her imagination, a sister she had missed for twenty years, maybe she should just play along. What could it hurt? If she was dreaming that meant Sydney was not dead, at least in that moment, and that was a welcome idea. Her choice became easy, she would not leave her sister. Even if she was only seeing Somer in a dream, she would enjoy her while she had her. Natalie got the feeling that this sister, this mirage, this dream, whatever Somer was, was as startled to see Natalie as Natalie was to see her.

Somer had never been a topic of conversation as Natalie grew up and her brother remembered nothing about Somer. Thoughts Natalie had of her were occasional, at best. Somer was not around for any memories. Natalie felt distress when realizing Somer knew her. She did not understand Somer had been visiting her on Earth, she didn't know all the ins and outs of it, but she knew enough to know that the situation warranted at least a bit of distress. She wondered if Somer had loved her family more than they had loved her. Perhaps this was not true though. Natalie knew, because of Somer, it was very possible to never see someone, their absence in your life all you had, but to still love them. It was possible to not talk to someone, to not interact with someone, yet to love them deeply.

Natalie's stomach turned at the possibility that Somer did not understand this. Losing Somer had been the greatest loss of Natalie's life. There was nothing Somer could ever do that would make Natalie love her less, and at the same time she could not love her more. The conviction had sticking power, and she suddenly believed this was her baby sister and she knew she loved her fully.

Four

"Somer," Natalie said, "What's inside that room?"

Somer visibly relaxed. Natalie had chosen to stay with her.

Somer was awash with thankfulness and Natalie could see it on

her face. Somer looked at her feet, her face flushed from sitting

through the tense moments as Natalie made her choice.

Bringing her head up only enough to be looking at the floor in

front of her feet, Somer smiled.

"Please, come in, this is my bedroom!"

Natalie stepped in, "What are all the doors for?"

"It's the best part of the Holding Place, Natalie. Behind

all these doors live people I love."

Natalie was curious about and fascinated by this answer

and wanted to know more. At the same time it seemed it was

more important to stay focused on Somer, at least in that

moment. Somer waited, but Natalie asked nothing more about

the doors. Somer supposed that must mean she had Natalie to

herself and had the anxious fear that she had to captivate

Natalie with something. She must make staying attractive or

intriguing. She must do anything she could to get her to stay. Somer's fear was that at any moment Natalie might choose not to stay. It was nothing short of miraculous that she was there at all. If Natalie was truly alive then Somer had no idea how this was happening. Natalie was in a position of great privilege to even have a choice.

"Would you like to look through my pictures?" Somer asked Natalie. Pictures, a visual reminder of the sister Natalie lost might keep her engaged, Somer thought. Her photo albums had pictures of her as a baby, when she had first come to the Holding Place, all the way through the present. Natalie sat on the floor and began to look through a mass of pictures. Somer lay haphazardly on the bed, tangled in a quilt her grandmother had made. The pictures prompted many questions from Natalie. Mostly asking who this or that person was, or where this or that picture had been taken, or how old she was in a certain picture.

Natalie became quite engaged in looking at the albums and Somer grew quiet. As if jerking awake from sleep, after Somer had been quiet for a while, Natalie looked at the bed and saw that Somer was asleep. Beside the bed was a wide-open window and Natalie could see it was dark outside. She crawled over Somer to look out the window. Stars were scattered across the sky. Natalie lay down beside Somer and rested her hand between Somer's shoulder blades. The skin Somer inhabited was the same skin she would have on Earth. She was starting to believe this was somehow more than a dream. Natalie had stopped asking why Somer had died, but now the question rose anew. All Natalie heard was silence as she reached over Somer to turn off the light on her bedside table. Then she, too, fell asleep.

Somer woke up early the next morning. The window was open and the sun was rising. A draft of breeze swept through the window. She did not remember falling asleep. She saw the picture albums stacked on the floor and remembered Natalie at once. She sat up and looked at the other side of the bed, for that second wondering if Natalie was still there. Natalie was there and she was asleep. Somer was excited and had the urge to wake her, but let her sleep and quietly got out of bed.

Somer tiptoed to the door that led to her grandparents' space. She softly opened the door and peered inside, seeing nobody. She went in and gently closed the door behind her and walked to the garden. There they both were, surrounded by vegetables.

"You won't believe this!" Somer said to them in excitement. She looked at their faces, enjoying holding such a wonderful secret to herself, and at the same time she was ready to share. "My sister is here. Natalie is in my bedroom, sleeping."

After an initial wave of disbelief, Somer's grandparents seemed to have the same thought Somer had at first, which was Natalie must have died. No matter how much of a joy this was for Somer, Natalie's death would have meant her Earth family had endured a great loss. They thought of their son, Somer and Natalie's father. They saw how losing Somer had torn him to shreds and did not know how he would bear the loss of another child. They also saw the pure joy on Somer's face and that was a wonderful thing to witness. They were both caught in the middle, walking a line between joy and sadness.

"Let's go introduce ourselves then," Grandma said, upbeat, wanting not a mar her granddaughter's joy.

"Yes, please come!" Somer turned, and they followed her to the door of her bedroom. Upon entering they found Natalie's eyes blinking open. Natalie remembered the night before and the dream of her sister. Natalie was disoriented. It had been a dream, hadn't it? Natalie saw Somer though, and she was surely awake at that point, wasn't she?

Natalie was unendingly frustrated at not understanding what was happening. She did not know what was going on. Was she dreaming, or wasn't she? She remembered Sydney's death and the cove, but what was happening now didn't make sense. Somer stood in front of her, along with an older man and woman.

"Natalie," Somer said, "I want you to meet our grandparents.

"Ok, hi," Natalie said, drawing out her words, lingering on both 'ok' and 'hi.' Natalie looked down at the quilt on the bed and pulled it around her. She tried to gather her thoughts in a rush.

"Natalie," the woman said, "Do you know what happened to you? Do you know how you died?"

"Grannie!" Somer said, "She didn't die."

"Somer, darling, that is not possible. Natalie must have died. People don't just visit the Holding Place."

"Actually," Natalie said, not knowing what to do other than go along with it, "I think she might be right. I don't think I died. I don't know what's going on. I might be dreaming right now." It was quite a bizarre situation, and she was not certain of what had happened, but she knew, awake, or dreaming, she had no recollection of dying.

"I saw a person visit when I first came here," Grandpa said. "There was a little boy who lived nearby, a couple of houses over. The boy was ten, but he died when he was just one. One day his father, who was living on Earth, was in a tractor accident. He was between life and death on Earth and when he was very close to death he came to visit his son in the Holding Place. For one day this boy's father was with him. Modern medicine saved him, however, and he went back to Earth, entirely. You should prepare yourselves, Natalie may not be here for long."

"No!" Somer cried. "I don't want to lose Natalie again."

Despite the fact that Natalie didn't believe this was happening, she made the choice to embrace it. Whether it was real or not was overshadowed by the fact she was experiencing it. She was alarmed that she might not be with her sister for long. If by some tiny fraction of a chance what was happening was real, she didn't want to lose it.

"If I go back will I even know I was here? Will I remember this?" Natalie asked.

"Natalie, I don't know," Grandpa responded. "I'm sorry." He grieved the loss his granddaughters had both borne.

"None of us knows what is going to happen," Grandma said, "let's enjoy it while we can."

"Stay," Somer said to Natalie, "please stay."

Natalie looked into her eyes, "Somer, I don't know if I can." Somer felt a sense of betrayal, as though if Natalie loved her enough she would stay no matter what, that nothing would be impossible. Natalie's frustration was high, and she was overtaken by the pain of this situation that indeed seemed very real.

Somer turned away with tears in her eyes. Somer had never known what Earth was like for the living. She was left out of the biggest commonality in the Holding Place, and that had been experiencing life on Earth. Somer wanted Natalie to stay, but even more than that, she wanted to go back with her.

Somer was going to lose Natalie, again. It seemed perhaps it didn't matter if Somer could make staying with her attractive and intriguing.

"Natalie, take me back with you! Let's just go back through the door you came in through. It will lead us back to Earth." Even as she said it, she knew it did not make sense. Somer had been to Earth many times, just going back with

Natalie did not mean she would suddenly be alive on Earth. Somer thought getting a taste of what it was like to have her sister know her, then to have her taken away, might be worse than her sister never knowing her.

Five

The door to their grandparents' space was ajar. They heard a knock at their front door. Grandpa opened the door and talked quietly for a minute, then he motioned to Grandma and she went to the door. They went outside, pulling the door closed behind them. Natalie and Somer looked at each other, both at a loss for what to say. Somer sat on the edge of the bed and Natalie paced the small room. They both felt that they should be using their precious time together to communicate, but they didn't. Their grandparents were outside for an incredibly long time, or so it seemed in their anticipation, but both Natalie and Somer were too much in shock to make an effort to do anything.

Grandpa and Grandma came back in. "There's just one thing," Grandpa said. He made eye contact with his wife and then looked at Somer, "We got something, just now, and it has to do with you Somer." Grandpa held an envelope in his hand and gave it to Somer. She looked inside. She poured a tiny gem into her palm. She held up the gem for them to see.

"I don't understand, what does this mean?" asked Somer.

"There's a legend that exists," said Grandpa. "I didn't think it was true."

Natalie and Somer looked at each other, and then back at him, expectant.

One day, according to the legend, it rained tiny gems in the Holding Place. It was as though a handful of glitter had been tossed it into the air, the sun catching the colors as they fell to the ground. It rained for only a minute, and the gems were very hard to find because they were so small. But some were found. The gem you're holding, Somer, is one of the gems found."

Natalie and Somer looked at the translucent blue gem, inquisitively. "If the legend is true, that is," he added, "this may be one of the gems. We have it on good authority the legend is true, and this is indeed one of the gems that fell."

"Where did the gems come from?" Natalie asked.

"You could say God, or the great creator, or the mother and father of us all. However you see the divine, the highest point of existence, that is who sent the gems. A power that is ever-present in our lives and has the potential to control everything, but doesn't. A power that has inundated our lives with goodness." Natalie was incredulous. Was this the God that people on Earth worshipped?

"Is this power the same God who is over the Earth?" Natalie asked.

"Yes, this power created all that is in existence."

Wondering how much the Holding Place was like Earth, and with the remembrance of the loss of Somer fresh in her mind, Natalie asked with a degree of distress, "Is there tragedy in the Holding Place like there is on Earth?"

"No, the Earth is where we truly grow, the sorrow and anguish on Earth teach us deep lessons, deeper lessons than we can learn here. The Holding Place is a place to recover, to be immersed in love. Everyone needs a break from hardship. No matter how important they are in our growth if they are constant they will break us. That is why it is different how long each person will stay here. Some people are broken by Earth. Some people need a longer amount of time to prepare to go back into it. Don't get me wrong, on Earth exists beauty unspeakable and that makes people ultimately thrive, but so do the hardships. But in the Holding Place is constant beauty unspeakable, and the trials are small. That heals us."

There was a pause, then Natalie asked, "Can I hold the gem?" Somer lifted her hand toward Natalie. Natalie carefully picked up the gem and closed her hand tight around it.

"As the legend goes," Grandpa continued, "People gathered up the gems, not understanding where they came from. The rain was so out of the ordinary they knew there must be something special about them."

"How did you get this one?" Somer asked.

"It was just now we got it. A man named Henry was at the door. He has been in the Holding Place a very long time. For him the Holding Place is the Final Place, which means he has memories from all his past lives. He said it was to give you a choice, Somer. Henry was one of those who collected gems the day it rained," Grandpa said. "We learned through Henry, today, that we were only seeing a tiny bit of the network that exists in Holding Place. There are many undercurrents running all around us that we do not know about. We did not know this could happen."

Though Grandpa's voice was questioning, he did seem to believe what he was saying. Somer felt like she would burst waiting for him to get to the message he was relaying. She was slightly bouncing up and down on the balls of her feet. Her arms were crossed and her eyes were wide with anticipation. She kept quiet though, and Grandpa and Grandma seemed unaware of her eagerness.

"According to Henry," Grandma said, "the gems are each a miracle. Miracles which those with the gems choose to use for loved ones."

Grandma paused and looked at Somer, whose expectation could not be hidden any longer. Natalie too was eager to hear how this had to do with a choice Somer had.

"He claims he just knew once they were in his hand," Grandpa said, with a bit of skepticism. "He knew they were miracles, all 6 of them. He knew in his hand he held great power. He knew they were to be used for the people of Earth and that he had to be extremely careful. Each life, each thing that happens on Earth creates ripples and waves that reverberate forever. Often what happens is minor, but even the most minor movement is impactful. We in the Holding Place can see things those on Earth cannot see. Our interference should be small, and only related to our tasks. But in his hand Henry had an invitation to interfere."

Perhaps it was the fact Grandpa was so close to telling them about the choice Somer had that pushed her as far as she could go. "What does this have to do with me?" Somer asked, on the border of talking very loudly and yelling. All three of them looked at Somer, as if just realizing how eager she was to hear the point of the story. "Yes, I'd like to know too," Natalie said in a much calmer way.

Grandpa went on, unflustered, "This man's task is to recognize the need for compassion and give it to those who need it. Henry has many descendants and you are each his descendants. He watches over his descendants on Earth, he pays attention to what is going on in their lives, although he has a great many of them. He was at the hospital the day you were born, Somer. He sensed an extreme restlessness in you. From the beginning you fought to stay alive and to be a part of the world. He saw great potential in your restlessness, in your fight, but saw you would not survive. He used one of his gems to splinter you at birth."

"What does that mean?" Somer asked, her confusion acting as a sedative.

"Somer, you are in the Holding Place as well as on Earth. You grew up in the Holding Place and at the same time on Earth. You were splintered into two the moment you died. Henry was there, the day you were born. Henry was there that day and understood you needed to be in the on Earth and Earth needed you in it. He knew you would always long for Earth, more than most. At the same time there was a woman who was in deep grief because she and her husband could not have a child. From the time she herself was a child she wanted to be a mother. Henry, having the task of giving compassion, was well attuned to her grief. That combined with your fight to live is what led him to use a miracle. When you were splintered, you were placed in the womb of this woman, her name is Margaret. You have the genetic makeup of this couple, and they named you, but you are a single being, living in two places. It was always meant for you to one day come together again."

"You mean I have an identical twin?" Somer asked.

"No," said Grandpa. "You are two halves of the same person, but you are both whole at the same time. You have different genetic makeups. You and this child who was born to Margaret, her name is Ella, are a single being, living in two places. Part of the miracle was one day you would have the chance for the whole of you to be on Earth. The gem Natalie is holding is the one responsible for the splintering.

"What does this have to do with a choice I have?" Somer asked, not understanding what he was saying and at the same time unsure if she could absorb any more information.

"Somer," Grandma said, "You can choose to join with Ella on Earth. You can live on Earth now, you don't have to wait."

Somer's response was sudden and it was as though it bypassed her brain. Despite the fact she did not really understand, she heard herself say, "Yes, I will go! My choice is yes!" She looked at Natalie, "We will be on Earth together Natalie."

"Not so fast," said Grandpa. "That's not exactly how it is going to happen. When you, if you go, you will not go back to knowing Natalie is your sister. You will be assimilated into Ella's body and mind and you will have no memory of your time in the Holding Place. Indeed, no one who goes back to Earth ever remembers the Holding Place or their old lives. Ella was placed in a geographically similar area to where your birth family is from, as you were from close lineages, so it is possible you and Natalie will cross paths, but certainly not a guarantee. Henry was waiting for when Ella died for you to know each other, if not joined back together. He sensed the turning point in her life Natalie was at and used a precious gem to bring her here to meet you, Somer. Your ancestor is looking after you. He has chosen to give you the opportunity to go back to Earth now, and a true miracle that would be, as it coincides with Natalie's visit here. Natalie will go back either way, and will not remember this."

"What happens if I decide to stay?" Somer asked, out of curiosity more than anything.

"If you decide to stay in the Holding Place, then when Ella dies, you will know each other and be together, you don't have to go to Earth now, Somer, you can stay in the Holding Place for many more years."

Both Somer and Natalie were quiet. "I'm going to go back and remember none of this?" Natalie asked after a few beats. "Where will everyone think I have been?"

"Time is different here," Grandma said. "It can be bent to fulfill needs on Earth. When you go back only seconds will have passed."

Somer was torn, living on Earth was what she had always wanted, but she did not want to lose Natalie either. Natalie, as if reading Somer's mind, said, "Somer, years on Earth are short. We will reconnect eventually. Not knowing each other does not mean we're not still sisters."

Seeing the struggles of Earth left Somer with only a surface understanding of what life was truly like, of what some of the horrors and tragedies that some on Earth may experience are. She thought like a child, the way a child dreams anything is possible. Very few children understand the complex chaos of life on Earth. It is something that can only be understood by living, unprotected, in a tangled world. In the Holding Place, Somer had a sense of security that was not present on Earth. For every raging beauty that came with being alive on Earth, there too was a raging cruelty.

Natalie understood this, and hoped if Somer chose to go to Earth, it would be worth leaving the wonder of the Holding Place. Natalie knew that Somer longed to be on Earth and wanted to go. There is more to existence than happiness, and it was a trade Somer was willing to make, for authenticity.

"Somer," Natalie said, "If this is what you want, and it's possible, maybe this is the best choice for you. I want to know you, but either way, I am not going to remember you. This is not about me though. It's about you. You won't remember me, but like I said, Earth years are short, and we will see each other again. If I could give you anything I would give you the Earth you so want to experience. Here it is, being offered, being handed to you."

Natalie didn't want Somer to go to Earth, but only because she didn't want Somer to experience the hardships of Earth. She felt protective of Somer, and felt that she would be most protected in the Holding Place. She had let Somer go years before, and now that she had her back, her feelings were maternal. This was Somer's choice though, independent of Natalie.

Somer was pensive even though she knew her choice would not waver from wanting to go. There was possibility that existed with indecision, however, that was attractive to Somer. 'Yes,' seemed very final. Once she was on Earth she was there. It was like jumping off a diving board. There is that moment you have jumped and are suspended in air. You have lost the ground you stood on but have not reached your destination. That place, that still place in the air, was where 'yes' would put her. For one terrifying second she would be suspended in the air, unable to go back, and plunging forward at a speed she had no control over. She knew her answer though, unequivocally, and so when she said, "Yes, I will go," it was filled with acceptance.

She jumped off that diving board and lost control of what was going to happen. She felt that there were things she should put in order, like she needed to clean her room, what would happen to her room? She felt the urge to say an emotional goodbye to Natalie and her grandparents and at the same time did not want to be emotional, as if she cried a little she would not stop.

"How will it happen?" Somer asked, "And how soon?"

"Henry asked us to summon him if you made the decision to go, he will know the procedure."

Everything was set into motion once Somer made that statement of assent. It happened in a matter of hours. Grandpa went to retrieve Henry. Grandma sat with Somer and Natalie in the garden and they talked. They talked as one might talk in end times. They told each other their secrets, their deepest fears and dreams, and the best and worst of their existences. Grandma wondered aloud who she had been in her other lives, as she could only remember the one she had just come from. They came to know each other in a way you could only know someone who you would never speak to again, or wouldn't speak to for many, many years.

Grandpa came back and told them Henry was on his way. Then Somer insisted on cleaning her room, so with

Natalie, she made it sparkle. Then Henry came. They went out to the garden.

Six

"Somer, you have made your decision, I hear," he said to her. They were all seated on the patio furniture. Somer was experiencing excitement and trepidation, both a sense of freedom and being trapped.

"How does it work?" Somer asked him.

"You and Ella will be combined into one. I'm not completely sure how it will work, I have never heard of this being done before. We will go to the great library. From there we will transition you to Earth. It will just be you and me. Are you ready? Somer said goodbye to each of them, giving them long hugs, emotional only on the inside. It seemed surreal, what was suddenly happening. Somer went to the library in a daze. The massive building was more like a community center than a library. It was near everybody in the Holding Place. No matter where someone lived, it was within walking distance. It brought people together from every nationality and language, and in the library, everyone understood one another, no matter the language.

They went into the empty room with marble floors. The room was small and intimate. In the room there was someone waiting for them. It was a woman holding an infant. But the mother and child weren't real, they were a mirage, Somer got the feeling she could stream her hand through them.

"Who are they?" Somer asked Henry. "This is Ella and her mother, right after Ella was born. This will be your mother on Earth. You won't remember the mother from your last life. You will have Ella's memory, this will be the mother you will interact with and love, the one you will turn to when you are sad, the one you will run to with open arms when all the beautiful things that will happen in your life, happen."

"Wait," said Somer, having misgivings "Am I going to be trapped inside Ella, like screaming to get out and being unable to?"

"No, Somer, you are Ella. You will simply be absorbed into her, become your complete self."

"Are you ready?" Henry asked.

"Yes," said Somer, "I'm ready."

"Will I be erased from my grandparents' memory?" she asked then, stalling, feeling nervous, even though she knew only her memory would be erased.

"No," said Henry.

"Okay, okay," said Somer, "I'm ready."

He put his hand on her forearm.

"Close your eyes," he said.

Then Somer felt a burning sensation in her arm. She wanted to tell someone to make it stop. She wanted to cover her arm with her other hand, but she was unable to move. In her mind her eyes bulged and her body tensed, but in reality she was still and quiet and her eyes remained closed. The burning sensation spread to her hand and up her arm and to her shoulder. Before the burning sensation went any further she had fallen asleep.

Then Somer woke up, but she was not only Somer. There was something dramatic, she was someone different. Somer had been shed of her body and consciousness and was in

Ella's body. Her mind was totally merged with Ella's mind, her thoughts not hers alone.

There was no separation of Somer and Ella, they were Ella. Ella felt something rough underneath her. She opened her eyes and sat up. She was wearing jeans, tennis shoes, and a red sweater. She looked at her hands and then put her hands to her face, her cheeks were round and her skin felt smooth. She ran her fingers through her hair. It felt silky. It was long and she pulled a strand of it in front of her eyes. It was blond. They had not had the same genetic makeup, but they were the same.

Henry told Somer she would lose her memory. This was expected. It was not expected that Ella would lose hers too. But then, the splintering and joining were only the result of miracles. It was not something that was routinely done, by any means. Ella did lose her memory. When they were merged, Ella collapsed. She awoke not knowing who she was or where she was.

Ella was scared. She dropped her hair and frantically looked around her. She stood up, nearly hyperventilating.

Nothing looked familiar. She did not know her name. She did not know who this person with blond hair was. It wasn't that she believed she did not have blond hair, she did not know what color her hair was, how long it was, or what its texture was. She saw woods to one side of her, and on the other side was a grassy hill which she could not see beyond. She was on the cusp.

Ella

Seven

Whatever I'm doing, that's my world. Like when I'm with my best friend and I know I can be myself, endlessly. When I am reading a novel that makes me implode with emotion. When my hands are wrapped around a hot mug of coffee and I'm dreaming to the depths of the ocean, swimming through both the dark and light of things. When I'm curled up in bed and I am crying and gasping for comfort. I have experienced them. I have been a part of them. I have breathed them.

I am not much different than a huge ball of rubber bands. The center, the core of me will never change but I have been wrapped tight with experiences. I can fall, but I will bounce back up, my landing will be soft. I am encapsulated, little me and a thousand protections around me. Thousands of hands are holding me. The rubber band ball is heavy. I can hold it only because it is me. It would be too heavy for anyone else, as their lives would be too heavy for me. Our lives are a weight beyond what can be measured. Everyone's life is heavy, perhaps with grief or happiness, or more likely, both. I can carry these rubber bands because just like it would be a struggle to carry what my physical body weighs, I can. It's not heavy when I carry it padded to my bones.

If I were to remove all these experiences and try to carry them in my arms I would have to surrender. As I regained my memory it was as though I carried each new experience in my arms, they were not yet a part of me. The more I remembered the more I had to carry. When I carry something too heavy I have two choices to avoid dropping it. I must reduce the load or increase my strength. I am grateful I have had the opportunity to do both.

As each past experience layered on I was able to resolve things as they came. At least they came slowly, rather than suddenly, rather than all at once. When I could resolve something, when I could take something in and understand, it was one thing less I had to hold. It was only those things I could not accept, and could not understand, that I could not hold. Sometimes, no matter how hard I hold onto something, I will drop it because I don't have the strength.

The experiences that were hard had been a part of me, and so I tried to carry them. As they were layered on one at a time I realized that out of all those hands that hold me, there are a few that were inappropriate. They touched me in bad ways.

It would have taken me a very long time to rip those bad ones out when they were a part of me, layered in with everything else. Before I lost my memory they were deep down. It would have been difficult to snip them and shimmy them out, without destroying all they touched. When they came to me fresh though, as new memories to hold, I saw how heavy they were and removed them with less consequence. The bad ones weren't many, but they were intense. With memories coming on as I built myself back up, I was able to heal.

The newfound nakedness of my life left me cold and mired, but at the same time weightless, as if I could run faster and jump higher than I had ever been able to. All of my memories were gone. The pictures, sound, and music that emanated from my very life were gone. I could not remember what happened before the field, until now. Now I believe I was always meant to take this journey.

The field was decked with wildflowers, and I ran. I kicked at things as I ran, I held my breath without meaning to, and no matter how much it hurt, I wouldn't let myself stop. I wanted the flowers to shrivel up and die away. I wanted the outside to match how I felt on the inside. Why was the sun shining? Why was nature happy? Why was there no hurricane surrounding me? Where was I going? Suddenly I fell, hard. I was lying on my back, looking at a yellow flower, and then I lost consciousness.

When I came to it was dark and I was getting cold. I remembered right away what happened and at the same time the headache and hunger hit. I rolled over on my side hugging my knees. It occurred to me I could hear and I wanted to hear myself talk. "Why am I lying here?" I was sure somebody would answer, a friend, somebody. No answer. The dark was becoming black. I suddenly panicked. I remembered the fall but could not remember anything else. Loneliness enveloped me. Maybe I was the last human alive. Certainly if I could not remember others the cord that tied me to them must be severed, I thought. I stood up and began to walk.

It was so dark I could not see my hand in front of me. Everything was gone from me and I wanted to walk. Walking was some kind of forward motion and even if I could not see, I was going to do just that. My eyes began to adjust to the darkness and stars and a sliver of moon were leading my way. I was knee high in grass. As it brushed against me I shivered.

I began to inhabit an alternate world. I was becoming someone different than myself. "What am I doing here?" I asked the air, hoping hearing my voice would bring me out. Nothing changed. I will scream, I thought, just scream. I took a deep breath and screamed as loud and long as I could. By the end of it all the breath in me was gone and the scream became soft. It was like being underwater and emerging just before it was too late. I collapsed to my knees as I tried to catch my breath. I wheezed and coughed and then I cried.

I didn't know I was crying until I felt the tears and then I really began to cry. I was all alone. Nobody knew me, and I knew nobody. I pounded the ground with my fist and gave myself up to despair. I slowly unfolded as I pressed down into the grass and flowers with my body and drifted off to sleep.

For the second time I awoke confused and alone, looking up at flowers. This time I remembered the last time I woke up and though my headache was gone, despair was in full force. This time it was light though, and the despair proved easier to fight. The flowers were pleasant. The need for food was pronounced. I thought perhaps I could construct weapons, hunt, kill, and cook. I knew this was an obvious impossibility, and my mood lightened with the absurdness. What could I do, but continue to walk?

I could scream again, I thought fleetingly, and then after quickly dismissing it, I pulled it back. Despite the certainty from the night before that I was alone, I knew it was much more of a certainty there were other humans in the world.

Maybe I could find one with food and maybe there was one nearby.

'I will scream again,' I thought, remembering the relief it brought me before and hoping it might truly be effective. I dropped my arms to my side, clamped my eyes shut and opened them wide. I was going to give it all I had. I took three deep breaths, moving inward and feeling peace. I screamed. My knees bent and I drifted down and then slowly came back up. I was gasping for air and then it was over and I smiled.

I could feel the lines on my face breaking loose, and I sighed. That was the first time I smiled in my whole life for all I knew. I put my hands on my hips, sighing again. I started to walk. I had not walked far when I decided one more time to scream. Justifying this choice I reasoned if someone heard me scream before they might need to hear me again to be sure to go in the right direction. I screamed the same way I had before, by the end I was gasping for air. My lungs were hungry and when I gulped the air I imagined them full and happy. God only knew if anyone was out there. God, I thought, I decided not to pull that one back.

I turned in a slow circle three times, in a fruitless effort to gain my bearings. It did not help. There was a stretch of forest a football field away. It was far enough that I could not see details. I could not tell if there were paths or friendly openings, or if I would be ensnared by renegade foliage. Still surrounding me were grass and wildflowers, knee high. I was torn in which direction to go. The forest had some promise but was scary. The field, which slowly slanted up, was more predictable, but something drew me to the forest. I turned in another circle, just to be doing something. I stopped for a few seconds after turning in a full circle, and then I turned one more time. In the middle of turning I became restless and started to walk toward the heavy band of trees.

The sun was high in the sky at this point and my sheer sense of being alone drove me, dulling the intimidation of the forest. My hands swung at my side, awkward with nothing to do. I reached the edge of the forest in less time than I thought it would take, after having a stretch of time musing over the loneliness of my hands. I clasped them together against my chest, where they remained, protecting me at the edge of the unknown. Confidence swept through me, and I walked to the right, scoping out the situation. After a hundred feet I found a trail leading into trees. Noticing my feet for the first time I saw I wore running shoes. The shoes were bright and shiny, blue with white stripes down each side. I began to run. The path was clear and I thought it was a well-used trail. I slowed to a walk after five minutes, or perhaps twenty-five. My sense of time was not very sharp.

"Where am I?" I asked aloud. "Who am I? What is my name? Why am I here? Why!?" Neither answers came nor any satisfaction from hearing my voice.

I would have thought what came next was a dream if I had not been solidly grounded in my senses: the smell of cinnamon. I bent down, the leaves when I swept my hands on the ground and the breeze through my hair were solidly real, so didn't the cinnamon have to be? With the cinnamon I tried not to get my hopes up, but it smelled delicious. Cinnamon gave me a feeling of nostalgia that I couldn't place, but it had to mean food, I thought hopefully, and perhaps, even happiness. I continued to walk, slowly and a little scared. I went off trail, and I couldn't see what was ahead of me. Please, I thought, please let there be something here for me. I saw the tree stump in the brush and picked up the steaming mug of apple cider that sat on it. I drank and it burned. Once again, this was odd enough that it seemed like it should be a dream, but I felt my tongue burn, it was real. The apple cider set my taste buds in motion, ready for food. There was no food though. I was angry there was no food.

I threw the mug down onto the stump and it broke into three pieces. I regretted it instantly, looking at the beautiful mug I had broken. It was a rich blue, handmade and glazed. It was strong, but not as strong as my anger. My anger was boiling over. I was angry I had nothing to sustain me. I had nothing to sustain any part of me. I looked at the blue and had a notion this mug was made specifically for me.

Then a reality hit me hard. All of my anger went away. I realized I could die. The void I felt in my stomach reminded me of my mortality. I could die in the woods. Unless I could find a way out, I was going to die. I needed help to survive.

I was mad at myself for breaking the mug, I was sure it had been given to me lovingly. It had been the one link I had to something outside myself. It was proof I was not so alone. If someone was out there looking over me then surely I would not die. I sat on the stump and looked at the mug, holding it together as it once was. It was so empty. I thought about water. I thought about how thirsty I was and how wonderful it would be if the mug was filled to the brim with water. I closed my eyes and pictured the cool mug on my lips. I imagined the sound of the first sip when the water would go down my throat and into my empty stomach. I stood up, determined not to die in the wilderness.

I said to someone, I did not know who, "I don't want to die and I don't know what to do. Please help me." I closed my eyes and behind my eyelids was beautiful color. I saw yellow, green, blue, red, purple, and more in infinite shades. It was exhilarating. It gave me an assurance that even if I did not understand what was happening, things would work out. The fear of dying was gone. I would not die. I would find what I needed. I also thought, however, if I did die, everything would still be alright. Better than alright. Things would be as they were meant to be.

All was silent. I could not bear to open my eyes to nothing changed, to the broken mug, the thirst, the hunger, and the weariness. I would not open my eyes until I figured out what to do next. I wanted to keep the perfect feeling tight to me. "I don't want to die. Please help me." I knew somehow I was sensitive to color, that it had a way of opening me up. The colors made me gentle. Surrounded by color I was open to learning. Surrounded by color I was patient, I did not want to scream, and I did not despair. Surrounded by color I was beautiful, like it was. There was a swell then, of hope. I opened my eyes, I did not know what I would do, but I had hope.

While my eyes were closed another mug had appeared on the stump. I held it in my hands, it had tomato soup inside. I drank it all, feeling the warmth right away. I looked back down on the stump and there was a small loaf of bread and another mug of tomato soup. I sat on my knees in front of the presentation and said, "Thank you, whoever did this. I am grateful. Maybe I will not die. Not yet."

I tore off a piece of bread and dipped it into the soup. I put it into my mouth and I felt safe. I ate every bit of it, drinking the last drops of soup and picking up the flakes of bread off the makeshift table. Just as the colors had, the food illuminated my dying spirit. I felt surrounded by light.

My mouth was dry and I imagined waves of clear, wonderful water breaking around me. I started choking, as if I were choking on the water I was imagining. I kept choking harder and harder until I could barely breathe. I thought of the hope I had just had. As I could breathe less and less I knew I could not guarantee anything. This was out of my control. I did not know where I was and I did not know who I was. I had mistaken hope for invincibility. Hope brought me joy and motivation to keep going. Assuming invincibility made me feel like I had control even when I had none. I did not want to be invincible! I didn't want to be responsible for stopping myself from choking. I would fail.

"Please, I still need you," I said to my earlier savior who provided me with food. "Please, make it stop, I can't." Then everything was still except for me as I gasped for air. I saw the water. It was a puddle. I remembered I had cupped my hands and taken a sip. How could this puddle of water hurt me? It was small and unassuming. I would not have even considered it could have power over me. How could I be so weak? How could it be so strong?

There was a tall, flat rock beside me. I felt myself lifted, as though I was floating in air. I thought the sensation must be coming from the lack of oxygen in my brain. The rock was in my periphery view but soon my back was turned to it and I was hurled against it. This surprised me, had I done this on my own accord? I hit the rock square in my back and the water, and what little air was left was forced out of me.

It took another few minutes but I could breathe again. I slowly slid down until I was sitting. My back was against the cool rock and I was still catching my breath. The rock was sturdy and was not going anywhere. It was planted into the Earth, unmovable, and something I could always come back to. It would be ever present.

The rock was a six-foot tall gray wall, four feet wide. It was relatively flat. It was a part of nature though and it had ridges and dents in it. If I were to run my fingers over it they would lift up and sink down with the variability that defined the rock's surface. The wall was rough all over. It was as though the surface of the rock was being shaken by an earthquake with a million tiny ripples on its surface.

I was not aware of what force had driven me to throw myself against the rock… or had I been thrown? I was not sure. The force was both gentle and powerful. It had been myself, but not myself. It was like every square millimeter of me was surrounded by strong air. It was air that held me effortlessly.

The rock saved my life when I was hurled against it. The memory of it would be power-filled, the way I was lifted off the ground, the way I seemed to float toward it, the way I was hurled against it. If I were I to leave and come back I knew it would somehow be able to save me again. I had the feeling I could leave courageously because I had a place that required no courage to come back to. It was a place where it had been alright to be weak. I could be bold because I could be meek in this place that was quiet and required no boldness. I could be loud because this would provide stillness. I could be anything because I could always come back to this place my life was once saved. I had nowhere to go, except here.

I walked to the stump and put my foot on it. The mugs sat in the middle of a rectangular outline that was on the stump. I bent down and saw two hinges on one side of the outline. There was a handle on the opposite side. It was a door and I was certain it had not been there before. I moved the mugs to the base of the rock and opened the door. I saw steps that led into the darkness.

I walked down the wooden steps, unafraid, and at the bottom there was a bare light bulb hanging from the ceiling, giving off a dull but adequate light. The little cove had a dirt ceiling, floor, and walls. There were many waist high stacks of three-ring binders. I picked up the binder on the top of the stack nearest to me. It was navy blue with no indication of what might be inside. I opened it up and saw each page was in a page protector. I smiled. Was this some massive school project?

The first page had a large block of very thin, horizontal lines of color beginning at the top with yellow and then the color changing easily from one to the other as they went down. The yellow gradually turned into orange, the orange gradually turned into red, the red gradually turned into purple, and the purple gradually turned into blue. The top line, which was yellow, was bold. I was drawn into the page and when I finally looked away, as though breaking a spell, I did not know how much time had passed. I flipped the page over and saw a picture of someone labeled, 'Margaret,' very young and very pregnant. On the opposite page was the picture of an infant labeled, 'Ella.'

I did not know who this baby, Ella, was, and I felt eager to see everything all at once. I set down the binder on the floor and picked up the next binder. The same block of color was there, and the same yellow line was bold. The next page had a picture of a baby, clearly the same baby as in the first binder I looked at. She had the same mole just under her right eye. It was labeled, 'Ella at one month.' I closed the binder and dropped it on the floor. I picked up the third binder. It had the same block of color and the same yellow line was bold. The next page had a picture of a baby, the same baby with the same mole and it was labeled, 'Ella at two months.' I closed the binder and returned all three to the stack. I knelt on my knees and counted the number of binders in the stack, my index finger touching each one as I counted. There were twelve. I saw that each stack but one was the exact same height, twelve binders per stack.

I moved on to the next stack of binders and opened the top one. The same block of colored lines was there. This time the second line of color, yellow with the slightest orange tint, was the one in bold. The next page had a picture of the same baby as the other binders, the same baby with the same mole, this one a little older. It was labeled, 'Ella at one year.' I replaced the binder and squeezed my way into the middle of the stacks. I picked up a binder on the top of a stack. The same block of colored lines was on the first page. About a fifth of the way down an orange line was bold. The next page had a picture of a teenage girl with the same mole. It was labeled, 'Ella at 14 years.' I turned back to the first page and counted the lines of color down to the bold line. The bold line was the fifteenth line down. Ella was in her fifteenth year of life.

I replaced the binder and squeezed back to the stack at the back of the cove, worried if I bumped into one stack they might all fall. This stack wasn't much, there were just two binders. I opened it and saw the same block of colored lines. This time the twenty-first line was bold. It was red and about a quarter of the way down. I turned to the picture of an older version of the fourteen-year-old. It was labeled, 'Ella at 20 years.'

I did not know who this young woman was, but I looked into her eyes and knew somehow she was connected to me. I laid the binder on the floor and then picked up the last one. I sat on the floor and opened it up. The same block of colored lines was there and the same red line was bold. It was the same young woman and she was laughing, but she also had guardedness in her eyes that I was unable to read. It was labeled, 'Ella at 20 and 6 months.'

This one was unfinished. There were no summaries and the days only went through the third of the month. That page said, "Ella was released from a psychiatric hospital." I remembered the faintest thing. I carefully made my way through the binders to the stairs, and then I ran up the stairs and out of the cove. I slammed the hatch shut. I looked at my clothes and remembered them being on the floor beside me. They had been balled up, pushed to the side, but I could make no sense of this memory. I walked to the rock and whispered a single word, "stillness."

I was dizzy and walked back to the stump and sat down. I noticed for the first time under my long sleeves my wrists were bandaged. Another small remembrance came back to me. I could taste it, the despair, thick with sadness, doubt, and dread, layered on top of each other. I did not know why I had felt that way. Something must have happened, but I didn't know what it was. I smiled, because I didn't feel that despair anymore. The stump was only a tiny part of what had been an entire tree. Inside the stump though held a whole world of someone's life, of Ella's life. What great things even the smallest and weakest could do, and I thought of the powerful puddle. I was Ella, I knew quickly and fully, and it was something I was sure of. The door was gone, but I was calm because I had received enough for that moment.

There was a stream near the stump. There were rocks scattered throughout it and small rapids within it. The color of the rocks ranged from dull silver to dark gray. Trees whose leaves were dying in a brilliant burst of color canopied the ten-foot wide stream. The banks on either side were ragged and they seemed to slowly sink into the stream, as if the stream were consuming them. It left me with the idea that over the years the stream would slowly consume more and more of the land.

Some of the rocks scattered were big enough and close enough to step on and it would be easy to make it to the opposite bank. Stepping on the rocks, I made it to the middle of the stream. I knelt down on a rock. Even as the leaves on the trees only clung to life, plants on either side of the stream were still lush green. As I looked down the stream I saw they closed to a point far down my line of sight. The trees lined the stream as far as I could see too, and as water flowed over the rocks tiny rapids were formed.

Dead leaves congregated at the rocks. They were stuck to the edges where the current pushed them into the rocks. The leaves clamored to be with the rocks but the rocks let them cling only to the outside, like a child at school desperate to fit in, who could not get past the periphery.

Instead of following the trail I decided to follow the stream. I picked up my favorite mug and took it with me. I was alone, but I knew the rock and stump were both there. They anchored me. There was something in the middle of the forest that stood solid.

I didn't know how long it took, walking on the rocks and on the banks, but I reached a road. I was on the inside of a slight curve. I stood with my toes at the tip of the asphalt and white line that bordered the road.

At first it was quiet but after a few seconds cars rushed past me, going in both directions. I stepped back, so as to be away from the danger. That meant no one could see me though, and I wanted to be seen. I stepped into the lane nearest me and faced the oncoming car. I heard the squealing of tires and wondered why I was playing with my life.

My mortality was fragile, the water I choked on earlier had shown me. I was not invincible. I was lost and alone. I needed people, I needed touch. I needed for someone to simply hold my hand. The need felt as critical as the need for food and water. Though standing in the road was dangerous, that was the fastest way I knew to get what I needed. I was desperate for another person.

From the car that skidded to a stop, a woman jumped out and ran up to me. She looked at me with concern. I must have looked dazed and dirty, holding my mug. "Are you okay?" she asked. Then with a hint of anger, "What on earth are you doing?" I found her eyes and looked at them, unblinking. She switched back to concern, "What are you doing out here? What's your name?"

It was as though my body had been waiting for hands to catch me. I felt my exhaustion. I dropped the mug and heard ceramic breaking. I collapsed, and she caught me.

Natalie

Eight

I was disoriented, and then it hit me, "No! Please God, no," I yelled, realizing Sydney was dead. My breathing was shallow and quick. I was so confused, had I just been here a moment ago? The thought left my mind quickly in my panic though. I was off the trail, and just started running in any which way, hoping it would get me to the parking lot. As I ran remembered my cell phone and pulled it out gratefully. No cell phone signal, I was sure I was becoming even more lost, but then I recognized a sign post and I realized that I was back on the trail. I knew I could make it from there.

I crouched to the ground for a moment, I was out of breath. I looked at my cell phone, I still had no signal. I stood up and walked a few paces, then began to jog. I didn't pass any hikers on the trail. I made it to the parking lot and got to Sydney's car. I only barely got signal. I didn't know if that was enough but I would try. I dialed 911 and it rang clearly. I was relieved. I looked around me as it rang. There were five other cars in the parking lot, but everybody must have been out on the trail.

"911, What's your emergency."

"Oh, thank you," I said with utter relief, "I am hiking at Stanley Point Trail with my friend, Sydney. She fell off a cliff and hit a rock. It killed her. I am at the trailhead right now, I didn't get signal on the trail. She is still out there. We need someone here now." I was talking urgently and felt like I was going to burst with pressure. My words were coming out very calmly though and that was shocking to me.

"I am sending someone out to you now. Please stay where you are. Are you ok?"

"Yes, I'm unhurt. I can't believe she's dead," I cried.

"Did you check for a pulse?"

"I checked for breathing and a pulse. There was nothing."

"The police and ambulance should be out there in 10 minutes. Stay on the line with me."

So I stayed. It was mostly silence but I was glad not to feel so alone. Then I heard sirens.

"The police are here. I'm going to go."

"Ok. Good luck."

The two police officers got out and I ran up to them. "My friend Sydney, she fell, she died."

"What's your name, ma'am?" he asked with expediency.

"My name is Natalie, we were hiking and got to a cliff, she lost her balance and fell to the bottom and hit her head on a rock. I checked for breathing and a pulse, but she's didn't have either. I did CPR, but there was nothing."

Then I heard more sirens. An ambulance pulled up. There were five of us. The parking lot that was empty now seemed bustling.

As soon as the EMTs got to us I told them the same thing I had told the police. I told them it was off the trail, but I could probably find it. The EMTs got their stretcher and bags and all five of us began to walk down the trail, rapidly. The whole way they asked me questions. I didn't know how they could ask me so many questions about such a simple accident. I was nervous that I would not be able to make it back to the cliff, I had almost gotten lost on my way back. When we reached the point where we went off trail, I began to concentrate more than it seemed I had ever concentrated on anything. I paid attention to everything we reached, searching my memory for just a short time before, when we had come this way. Then, we were there. We were at the cliff. It must have taken us 45 minutes. They followed me to the peak and I pointed down.

"There she is," I said, my calm exterior fading, "There's Sydney." She looked exactly as I had left her. Now, the EMTs took the lead, followed by me, followed by the police officers. The EMTs made it down surprisingly fast to be carrying bulky bags and a stretcher. I was running on adrenaline. The terror was exhausting but I was wired.

The EMTs quickly put the stretcher and bags down and felt for a pulse. 'What if I'm wrong?' I thought with a sudden shock. 'Maybe she's still alive.' I had an eruption of hope that was quickly dashed when the EMT said, "No…," affirming her death, "Let's put her on the stretcher." Everything went very fast after that.

This time I was in the back, my mind flooded with thoughts of what would come next. I didn't know Sydney's family and I wondered if it would be possible to not face them. The EMTs went faster than I did and were very competent at finding their way back to the trail. I kept up for a while but then fell behind. At one point I stopped and watched them round a corner until I could no longer see them. I wanted to stay in the woods. I didn't want to face what was next. Then, in a perplexing panic I ran to catch up and for the rest of the time they were within my sight.

When we got back to the parking lot they loaded Sydney into the ambulance. I had Sydney's backpack and I pulled her keys and cell phone from it. I found 'Mom' in it and called.

"Hi Syd!" the voice said with enthusiasm. I was quiet.

"Sydney?"

"This isn't Sydney," I said, pained, "this is her friend, Natalie. We were hiking. There was an accident. I think you should go to the hospital." My stomach was clenched tight as I said those words.

"Is Sydney okay?" the woman asked in alarm.

"Well," I said hesitating, "Not really."

"Can I talk to her?" she said with forcefulness.

"I think you should just go to the hospital."

"I want to talk to Sydney," she said, urgently.

"You can't."

"I want to talk to Sydney," she cried.

"I'm so sorry, Sydney… died… in an accident. I really think you should just go the hospital." I talked so quietly I wondered if she had heard me. But I knew she had when she started to cry.

"Who is this?" she asked, sharply.

"My name is Natalie. Sydney and I were hiking together."

"I'm on my way, please meet me at the hospital, Natalie."

I didn't know why it hadn't crossed my mind that I should go to the hospital, but I very much did not want to. The ambulance had already left and the police were standing there, waiting for me to get off the phone.

"Do you want us to take you to the hospital?" One of the police asked.

"Yes, please," I said, in a desperate whisper.

Sydney's mother and brother were already at the hospital when I got there. I saw no sign of Sydney, but one of the EMTs was talking to them. In my mind, I shrunk to a quarter of my size, a child who was terrified of punishment. It seemed like I was going to be in trouble, though I had done nothing wrong. I couldn't help but feel like I was to blame, and would be blamed.

I let out a cry, and all of them looked at me.

"Are you Natalie?" the woman asked.

"Yes," I said, feeling very uneasy.

"My name is Martha. I'm Sydney's mom. She seemed remarkably calm. "And this is Steven," Sydney's brother.

I didn't say anything at first. I didn't understand why her mom was so calm. Then I realized she was in shock. Steven had more emotion on his face, and was quietly crying. "We need to see my sister," he said. The EMTs took them away, and I went to the police station with one of the officers to make a report. When I went home that night, I was too tired to sleep, although it was all I wanted to do. I couldn't cry. I lay in bed all night, getting up every once in a while and eating ice cream, numbing the numbness.

I lived alone, and that night I both wanted to, and didn't want to be alone.

Ella

Nine

I used all my willpower to command my brain to wrench my eyes open. I was overwhelmed by white brightness. I was in a hospital. It was the opposite of the dark forest I had been in. There had to be people nearby. I saw a button you could push to call for help. I pushed down the button and then repeatedly pressed it down. A nurse came in and told me to stop pushing it, that I only had to push it once for them to hear me. In a mood so elevated I was childlike, I pushed it down again and again. I locked eyes with the nurse until she came over and pulled my hand off the button. I sighed. My profound need for human connection was very slightly relieved.

I had it in my mind that hospitals were bad places. A hospital was where someone went in alive and came out dead, right? The harsh lights comforted me though. If the lights were this blinding and the white floors this clean then surely I was safe. Only seconds had passed since the nurse came into the room and I understood it could not be good to get on the bad side of one of the first people I ever remembered seeing, and I apologized.

"Do you know how you got here?" she asked. Sleepiness took me over. I had to have been drugged, my eyes kept closing. My thoughts were unclear and when I spoke I slurred my words.

"I fell down in the road," I saw a look of worriedness on her face just before I closed my eyes again and fell asleep. I drifted off barely, and when I woke up, the phrase began to play in my head repeatedly, 'Do you ever see anything other than bodies?' This had been part of my dream, but I couldn't remember any more of it. But it was a question I quickly could not get out of my mind. Then the question jumped from only my dream to vague memories. I had the feeling I had asked myself this many times. I didn't know what it meant, but I imagined this being asked forcefully, demandingly, and angrily. I sat up in the hospital bed, anxious. I fell back against the pillow and wondered what "Do you ever see anything other than bodies?" could mean. The question disturbed me but was energizing. Something to do with my mind had presented itself to me. I was in need of that, of something to do in the white room.

In my mind was chaos. I liked this word. I said it out loud so I could feel the word on my lips, one word that could cover everything. There was so much in my head and I did not know what to do with it. It was everywhere, chaos. The dream and the question it brought up, the forest, the mugs, the stump, the cove – they were all a mass of chaos in my mind. It was a mass that swallowed me. Only by repeating, "chaos," did I feel some comfort. It was a word that was bursting at the seams. It cut through the fog, and like the stump was a doorway to much more, that one word was a doorway to respite. It was small, this word, but big enough to pull everything inside, to vacuum seal it in a jar, just for a while. I took the chaos and set it on the table beside me. I would deal with it later.

With the chaos gone I began to feel other things. My attention was drawn to the fact I wanted another blanket, to use the bathroom, to get something to drink, and to laugh. Feeling much lighter than I had before, I began to make things happen. I was able to yank the needle out of one arm and the blood pressure cuff off of my other arm, initiating a loud beeping noise. I went to use the bathroom, blood from my arm leaking onto the floor and into the bandages on my wrist. At the sink I cupped my hands together to drink water out of the faucet. I did not have an extra blanket, so I spread a towel over the bed. I attempted a smile, but it felt empty.

Realizing I was quite exposed in my hospital gown I took it off altogether. I wore nothing but the fresh bandages on my wrists, I didn't want to look underneath them. I pulled the blanket off the bed and wrapped it around me, blood still dripping from my arm where the needle had been. I felt like an ancient toga-wearing Roman or an American bride. I felt very far from either, but if I had to choose one I had a much better chance of being a bride than an ancient Roman. Armed with this knowledge I waltzed into the hallway, which was not dissimilar to an aisle. I easily found the nurses' station and saw the nurse who had come into my room earlier.

"No," I said to the back of the nurse's head, "I don't know who I am or how I got here. Do you know?" She had swiveled toward me in her chair while I was talking and then swiveled back around to the other nurse. She held up her index finder as she swiveled back around to tell me to wait a minute. She spoke quietly to the other nurse, at length. "Excuse me," I said finally, "Can you tell me what's going on?" The nurse glanced around, "Give me just a minute," she said. She spoke to the other nurse for a few moments more and then stood up and walked toward me.

"I'm sorry," she said, "I think it would be best for you to talk to a doctor. I'll call the doctor for you."

"Thank you," I said, and I began to pace up and down the empty hallway. My feet were bare and I clutched the blanket as I walked. Every time I passed the nurses station I stared, as if that would somehow give me information. Sometimes the nurse who had come to my room would watch me pass, sometimes she gave a quick glance, and sometimes she did not look at all. The other nurse paid me no attention. They were apparently not worried I no longer had my IV in.

Finally, a round man in a striped green dress shirt and white overcoat showed up and pulled up a chair in the nurses' station. He spoke to the nurse who had checked on me while the other nurse went to check on patients, all of whom were quiet in their rooms, except for the occasional television that was on or visitor with them. I kept walking though I was feeling progressively weaker. Finally, overcome with tiredness, I went back into my room and lay down on my back, still clutching my blanket.

I fell asleep again, but heard a kind voice speak my name. I opened my eyes to find the doctor looking at me in a friendly manner. I sat up. "I need something to eat," I told him, "I want to talk to you, but I need something to eat."

"Of course, the food here is not bad, let's see if we can get you something to eat from the cafeteria," he said, and pressed the button to the nurses' station. When the nurse walked in he asked, "Julie, could you get Ella something to eat? Do you know what they have today?"

"Let me get her a menu," Julie responded. While Julie was gone the doctor introduced himself as Dr. Richards. Quickly, Julie came back holding a half page menu in her hand. "Just circle what you want," she told me. "They just finished serving lunch, so it should all be available." From the menu I chose a cheeseburger, green beans, a macadamia nut cookie, and sweet tea.

After the nurse took the menu to send for my food, I looked at the doctor and said, "Somebody knows me."

"You told us when you came in that your name is Ella, but that's all you knew. Is there anything else you can tell me now about who you are?"

"What's wrong with me?" I asked, not answering his question. There was no way I was going to tell him about the binders. It seemed too bizarre.

"When you came in yesterday evening you were disoriented. You did not know anything about who you are.

You were also very emotional. I was hoping once you had some sleep things would make more sense for you. It sounds like you still don't know who you are or what happened though."

"Nothing," I said. I remember what happened right before I came to the hospital but that's all. "Will I start to remember things?" I became angry, it rushed at me like a sudden rainstorm. My eagerness for his response was an out of body experience. For me, everything hung on his answer.

"Just because you don't remember now doesn't mean the memories aren't there," he said, consolingly. I silently thanked God. "Let's start with what you do remember, from right before you got here."

"I remember stepping in front of the car, the woman getting out of the car, and I remember fainting. I thought stepping out in front of a car was the only way to get someone to stop. I know that wasn't the smartest idea."

"Okay, good," he said, "and do you remember anything before that?"

I hesitated, choosing my words. I thought my story of the cove might seem a bit off. The soup, I would tell him about the soup. That did not seem quite as crazy, did it? "I remember the stump, the one that had food laid out on it. It had apple cider and then tomato soup and bread, it was delicious."

The doctor looked skeptical, "Are you saying you were in the middle of the woods and found a tree stump with food laid out on it for you?"

"Yes," I said, "Hot food." He flashed me another skeptical look.

"Was there someone out there, a house nearby, perhaps? Someone who could have put the food there?"

I hesitated again, feeling like I had said too much. He probably thought there was something wrong with me. "No, I know it doesn't make sense, but it's what happened, I'm telling the truth."

"I'm glad you can see this does not make sense. That's important because your memory of what happened is illogical and unlikely. Hot food does not stay hot for long, and of course, there's the question of who put it there and why it was there."

I studied Dr. Richards. His face was clean-shaven and his hair was thick and white. Somehow I trusted him. It seemed that he both respected me and was taking me seriously.

"How strange," he went on, with inquisitiveness. "Memory is tricky. What we remember is clouded and shaped by the many different things going on inside and outside of us." He looked away from me, thinking deeply. "We may not be able to fix the warped memories, but as long as we can objectively look at these memories we won't get lost in them." His assumption that the meal on the stump was a warped memory made me doubt myself, but I knew I was right. "I don't know why you don't have your memory right now, but we will work on figuring it out."

It was difficult, no, impossible, to take a family history if you could not remember your family. This led to a complete physical, blood work, and an MRI. The physical was less invasive than I expected, the blood taking cringe-worthy, and the MRI seemed overboard. I had a psychiatric evaluation too, due to my wrists. The results of it all turned up nothing out of the ordinary.

I was in a difficult situation. There was not anything tying me to the hospital, yet I had nowhere to go. I was terrified of leaving without a place to go so I pretended not to be as well as I was.

As the days passed I grew to be a part of things. One nurse even brought me clothes to wear. Because the staff understood that without my memory I had no place to go they let me be complacent. At first, that is, they let me be complacent. The lack of effort to speed me out, at first, seemed mutual.

When I was there almost a week the doctor came in and explained I was ready to leave and stay in touch on an outpatient basis. "Do you know how expensive it is to be hospitalized?" he asked, as though he were trying to convince me that leaving was a good idea. The logical part of my mind considered this, perhaps I should worry about something practical, like money, I was soaked in fear though.

"The Social Worker will be coming in to talk to you," he told me. The Social Worker, a person I had not met, nonetheless represented something I did not want. Though this may have been a perfectly nice person, a bias existed right away. This would be the person to make me do the last thing I wanted to do. "Even though you do not have your memory back," the doctor continued, "I feel you are ready to go. I cannot say if, when, or to what degree your memory will come back. I'm sorry, this is no longer the ideal place for you to be."

Later that day a Social Worker named Marcus came into my room and explained I was in an unusual situation, as though I did not know this. He asked if I had any thoughts on what the next best step for me would be. I felt like throwing my jar of chaos at his feet, for the jar to break and the chaos to pour out, and to let him deal with it.

"No," I simply said, not making eye contact. I could not have been more upset and understood the saying, 'scared to death.' This could be the death of me, I thought. I had no money, no home, and no loved ones. The cove seemed less and less real the more time I spent around people I knew would not believe me.

Then, in fit of gumption, I pushed up my sleeves and showed him the bandages on my wrists. I had refused to look at my actual wrists when they had changed the bandages each time, so I didn't completely know what I was saying, when I asked, "Do you know what happened?"

"No, Ella, not exactly." Those are serious cuts and while they are fairly recent they were healing when you came in and they had not needed stitches. There were no patients reported missing from any nearby hospitals. It is a sign of distress, but the doctor said you seemed physically and mentally well enough to leave. Are you feeling depressed?"

"Oh, no, I'm not, do you think… I did this to myself?"

"Yes, The doctor believes the cuts are self-inflicted. But I don't know the circumstances around the incident in which they occurred."

I hung my head, in shame, or perhaps, in fear.

"I'm fine," I told him. "I must admit, I'm not happy with my circumstances, but I'm not depressed. Has anyone reported me missing from anywhere?"

"No, I looked into it though. I checked with surrounding police in addition to hospitals, and no one, at least not nearby, reported you missing."

"I really don't want to send you to a homeless shelter, and given your loss of memory the doctor does not think that's a good idea. I have talked to a foster family who has taken in older children. Even though the doctor believes you are over eighteen, this could be a good temporary match for you, they are willing to take you in, temporarily and unofficially, until we can make more appropriate arrangements."

It sounded like the worst idea I had ever heard. I was not a child… at least as far as I knew. According to the binders I was 20. I willed other possibilities to enter into my mind, but nothing came.

"Isn't someone looking for me?" I said in frustration.

"It's possible Ella, but nothing has been reported."

"I think I might need to stay in the hospital," I told him.

"Ella, I have talked to your doctor, and we are going to need to move you out of the hospital. You are physically ready to go."

I considered screaming but instead very calmly asked, "What can you tell me about this family?"

They had 2.5 kids, he told me, unsuccessfully attempting to lighten the mood. "Just kidding!" he said cheerfully. "They have two children and a dog. My dog is like my child," he chirped. My mood became more morose the cheerier he became. Their names are Cale and Kristen de Angelo and their children are 10-year-old Hazel and 16-year-old Will. They're a great family. Cale's an obituary writer and Kristen's a teacher."

"What kind of profession is an obituary writer?" I asked, critically.

"He loves it," Marcus responded, "He's got quite the passion for it. I have gotten to know them because of the other foster children they have taken in."

"I am not a foster child," I told him stiffly, "I'm an adult."

"Of course you are," he said, without much conviction. "This is going to be a great fit." I did not know Social Workers were psychic, I thought, unhappily. This was my only option though, and so I would do it.

After the Social Worker left, obviously quite pleased with himself, I was alone again. The room was humid with the safety I wanted so much to cling to. Now though, unlike before, the humidity was making it harder for me to breathe. My breaths came at uncertain intervals, with occasional gulps to take in the air I withheld. The thick air was holding me up, and it was as though I was on a tightrope, high in the air. The slightest movement and I would plummet to my death. That was what would happen, certainly, when I was forced to leave the hospital. "I cannot fall," I thought over and over.

It was decided by the psychic Social Worker I would leave the next day. The next morning, I dressed in the clothes one of the nurses had brought me, soft jeans and a plaid shirt. It was time to leave.

Ten

I knew right away it was going to be a challenging fit,

beginning when I realized their Golden Retriever was named

Will Jr., after the 16-year-old son. Really, I was looking for

reasons to dislike them. Looking for the negatives made it easy

to ignore the positives. Cale and Kristen de Angelo were slow

to gain my appreciation. One of the first things Kristen did was

try to take away my grocery bag of pajamas, underwear,

toothbrush, and toothpaste. She apparently did not realize I was

one thread away from a panic attack, because she sure did

persist. That was not okay with me, and I loudly told her, which

was a bad way to handle it.

Kristen looked upset when I raised my voice and told

her never to get near me again. Because the panic subsided just

a bit when I told her this, I continued. I went on to say that their

house was a last resort, that I had no other options. I also threw

in the questions of what kind of person loves obituary writing

and why would you give your dog the same name as your child.

Cale had greeted me and then went into his office to work. When I said this he came into the kitchen and calmly said, "Ella, why don't you come into my office and I will tell you why I love writing obituaries."

His office was large and the walls were filled with frames holding documents, such as his college diploma and an award he had received from the newspaper. I sat down across from him as he sat at his desk. I saw frames facing him, they must have been family photos. His computer sat on the left side of his desk, black and sleek. On the right side were stacks of file folders and papers. There was a large window to the left of the desk. Behind him were shelves lined with books.

"When a person dies," he stated as I recoiled at the mention of death, "their life surpasses them. They are no longer moving, changing, fluid, and indefinable. When a person dies they become a statue, unchanging and defined. They do not freeze in the position they were last in or into the person they last were. They become a shell that holds every experience, every good and bad thing they have ever done, their faith, their work, their friends and family, their hopes, and their realized and unrealized dreams." The poetry of Cale's words grounded me.

Cale looked at me, gauging my interest, as this was clearly something he could go on about. He sighed, "Who they were, how endless and complex and fascinating each and every person who lived and died was, it is this I love. I can barely touch the essence of each soul, but I like knowing when I write out a person's name, age, survivors of the deceased, and funeral arrangements, I am holding an entire world in one paragraph."

After he stopped his monologue he paused and then, "Of course," that's not all I do for the paper, but that's the part I love, that's the part I claim."

It was a strange profession to be passionate about, but his passion was catching. Cale told me he was writing a book, with permission from families, of local people who had died and their stories. "Everybody has an interesting story, but not everybody's family wants to share it." Cale asked me if I would like to read some of the stories and I said yes.

As the first week at the de Angelo's dragged on, I wanted to leave many times, but Cale's stories kept me, they gave me something to look forward to. I loved the stories Cale was making into a book. In learning about the people it seemed that I knew them. It was almost like making friends. It was sad to think my past life might be gone forever. I grieved during that time, for a loss I did not know, but knew I had experienced.

One of the stories I read was about a man named Abraham Wilson, who died at the age of 97. His family said every once in a while he would say, "I have outlived everyone, I'm ready to go." I wondered what it would be like to know the people you grew up with were all gone, maybe even long gone. Then I realized in a way, that's how it was with me. All the people I had once loved were gone. The past had shaped me, yet I only had wisps of it.

Abraham could have reached back into his memory and brought those people back to him but I could not find them at all. It was a lonely feeling and I was filled with regret for the people I did not say goodbye to, those relationships I could not remember but knew had been left unfinished. Abraham showed me that we leave this world alone, our final breaths are ours alone. Only God who inhabits us is with us. I did not know what happened after death, but there must be a reprieve from the loneliness of the world. There must be something beautiful waiting for us. It was a beauty I longed for.

I read all the stories Cale had written for his book. When Cale saw my passion for his project he hired me on. He would pay me in food and board and a little spending money each week. I could stay there as long as I wanted and help Cale with his work. This seemed overly generous, and I appreciated his willingness to help me out.

When I reminded Cale he did not know if I had even graduated from high school, he said, "Ella, I'm not worried at all if you're smart enough, you drink words, you understand words." He was right, too. The words from the stories I read crashed over me and mixed me up, they drenched me and took me to another world where I would leave soaking wet and dripping with newness. In the stories I found the histories and families I did not have.

Each person's story had a picture with it. Each picture was of the person as a child. Cale told me he had asked for a picture of each person as a child because while writing the stories he wanted only the child staring out at him. Adults were too guarded, their personalities set and unwavering. A child is open and a child's story is just beginning.

The pictures were my favorite part. In the beginning I removed each picture from the story it was paper-clipped to, knowing the back of the picture was labeled with the name of the person it belonged to. I avoided looking at which stories the individual pictures were attached to. Without looking at the names on the back of the pictures, I tried to match each picture with the story it belonged to. The only clue I had was the gender of the child in each picture and how old the photograph was. I would set each picture on the desk, my fingers holding the edges down tight. Each picture had a great deal of character. They were all taken in different places, a living room, a kitchen, outside. Often there were many things in the background. Many times, there were other people in the picture.

I looked into each face, trying to figure out traits and imagining what future experiences would behold this small child. There were ten pictures, eight completed stories, and two incomplete ones. I tried to figure out traits of those pictured and after I made my guesses, I fully re-read the stories. I internally cheered when I made a correct deduction. Even when I deducted wrong, I was grateful to learn more.

Cale had given me two sets of notes to begin putting into stories. One set of notes was of a man named Jerry who had died of a heart attack at the age of sixty-seven. In his picture, he looked to be about 5-years-old. He wore a blue collared shirt on his tiny frame, untucked, and jeans. He was barefoot. His hands were on his head, as though he were holding an invisible hat on. Sitting on the floor in the background was a little girl in a green, polka dotted sundress holding a doll and looking as though she were talking to it. In the corner of the picture was the bottom of a long skirt as well as a leg and foot of someone walking. A second later and it would not have been in the picture at all. In the background was an old-fashioned television, the kind you had to turn on with a knob.

The next set of notes was about a girl named Leah who had died of Cystic Fibrosis at the age of seven. The picture was of two children squished together with people who must have been their grandparents. It was an uncentered photo in front of a simple white marble fireplace. There was a fireplace screen behind them and Christmas stockings hanging on the corners of the screen. On the left was a little girl in white long-sleeve nightgown. She was leaning against the man, their faces connecting. Her little hand, a loose first, sat on his shoulder. His arm was around her waist and enveloped in the folds of her nightgown. The hand around her waist covered her other hand completely and his hand looked like it was floating in a sea of fabric. His skin was far darker than hers and the contrast made him look more weathered than he might have otherwise. His navy and red plaid shirt contrasted with the white of her nightgown. He was happy, looking weary, but quietly filled with joy at the situation he found himself in. Next to the grandfather was a young boy, laughing. He was in between his grandparents. His arms were around his grandparents, and he was outfitted in pajamas that were a deep green. He looked to be pulling his grandmother toward him. She had her left hand out, grasping something, as if to keep from being pulled over. Her hair was mostly gray but you could see it had once been dark, like the others'. She wore a white pullover sweater that was loose and as comfortable looking as the girl's nightgown. She sat with her legs folded underneath her, making her the tallest one. It was a picture filled with joyfulness. In keeping with Cale's thoughts on the openness of children, the faces of the children were innocent and trusting, while the faces of the grandparents were harder to read.

Every adult was once a child. By looking at a child you could see his or her goodness and infinite worth wide and clear, unblemished by the turmoil of the years. Behind each picture was an abyss. The notes told the stories, but there was a deeper story too. The deeper story was one Jerry and Leah had in common. They were both human with strengths and faults. They were both imperfect but had been fiercely loved. They still lived, even after death, through the times when they were thought of and talked about.

Cale walked in then, "It's an investigation Ella. All of these people's stories are like solving a case. The end result is the written story and everything leading up to it is evidence. There is much more to it than just talking to the families. There is the talking to friends and co-workers, the research of schools, work, family, and anything else that comes up."

After spending a week on Jerry's story and a week on Leah's story, and more time editing other stories Cale approached me with a new possibility. "Maybe you could focus on one story, from beginning to end. By that I mean starting from scratch, doing the research, interviews, and writing the story out. I have one that might fit you well."

"Yes," I said without hesitation, "I would love to do that!"

"How about this one?" Cale asked, holding up a picture I had not yet seen. It was a picture of a little girl named Sydney.

Eleven

Sydney Everett was born and raised in Carlton, North Carolina, the town I lived in with the de Angelos. The picture her mother gave Cale was taken in Carlton on a day when it snowed. According to a note on the back of the picture it was the biggest snow of Sydney's life at that point. In the picture Sydney was encapsulated in pink. She was bundled up in pale pink sweatpants and a warm looking coat with pink sleeves and a striped blue, pink, and teal front. Her gloves were pink with some kind of cartoon on the front of them. Her toboggan was white with pink horizontal stripes that had a long tail that hung down to the side. A scarf, striped black and white was the only thing that had no pink in it. It looked like a last minute addition, hastily put on when realizing how cold it was, and not a part of Sydney's wardrobe. The tail of the toboggan was tucked into the scarf. Her cheeks were rosy. The background was simple, snow covering everything. She looked thrilled to be in that winter wonderland.

There were vague notes Cale had on Sydney. She was 24 when she died. She had fallen off a cliff on a hiking trip. She was survived by her parents, Martha and David, an older brother, Steven, and a younger sister, Courtney. She had gone hiking with her friend, Natalie, who had been the one to report the fall. There was a brief statement that Cale had scribbled, 'Sydney was greatly loved, please be respectful, help us keep her alive with your words. –Martha.' The notes said Martha was the primary contact and gave the number for the Everett house. In the notes was also Natalie's number, and I was equally intrigued about calling her.

I was nervous about calling Martha Everett. Cale had not told her I would be doing the story and she would be expecting a call from him, not me. I was in Cale's office while he was at work at the newspaper. My hands shook and as I dialed the number I sideswiped a 7 when I meant to press 8. I had to start over and almost got it wrong the second time. I stood quickly as the phone began to ring, sending the office chair rolling backward. I prayed nobody would answer. As it rang a deep dread grew in my belly. I had no idea what I would say to Martha, whose child had died.

My mind filled with the shock that Cale knew what he was doing and I knew nothing. As the third ring came to an end and the fourth started I felt incrementally better, it was going to go to their answering machine. Halfway through the fourth ring somebody picked up, either Sydney's father or brother. I was completely quiet as he repeated "hello" several times. After he hung up I immediately hung up and picked the phone back up and dialed again.

"Hello," I said eagerly, "I'm sorry, I was tongue-tied before. Cale de Angelo, who I'm working with, was given permission from Martha to research her daughter, Sydney's, life, and write about it." My words were a blur, flying into the phone. I wanted to get everything out before I lost my nerve.

There was silence and then, "Oh Sydney is, was... is, my sister. Martha is my mom, you should talk to her. If you leave your number I will give it to her." I silently cheered, happy it would not be me to call and be awkward about the whole thing next time. All I had to do was wait and answer the phone. Then I quickly realized I would have to be at the phone when she called. I decided to stay in the office.

Martha did not call for hours and I was on edge because of it. I somehow managed to not come up with any questions to ask Martha during that time, though that would have made things much easier. I sat in Cale's office, arranging and rearranging the desk. The stapler, tape, hole puncher, thumbtacks, and everything else were all neatly lined up. Just when I was about to give up the phone rang.

I answered and heard, "Hi, I'm calling to speak with Ella."

"Yes, hi, this is Ella. Is this Martha?"

"Hi Ella, my son told me you called. You're working with Cale de Angelo?"

"I am. Thanks for calling me back Martha. I'm so sorry about your daughter, Sydney, I can't imagine what you must be going through." Then there was silence. My thoughts began to derail with that silence. 'Of course I did not know what this grieving mother was going through. Why did I say that? What if she hangs up on me? She is going to hang up on me,' I thought. I willed her to say something, anything.

"I was expecting to hear from Cale, I did not know he had someone working with him."

"I have only recently begun working with Cale. I was hoping to ask you a few questions."

"Sure," she said, "go right ahead."

"What was Sydney like?" My inner monologue began running again. Was that question too broad, too general? All I heard was silence.

Then, "She was beautiful, inside and out. She was just Sydney. There was no one like her and there is no one who will ever be like her."

I waited, but she did not say anything more. I scrambled for another question.

"Um, ok, thanks, um…"

"How many of these biographies have you done?" she asked.

I closed my eyes and said, "Well, none." Was she hearing from that response that her daughter was not important enough to warrant the expert? I hoped not.

"What happened to Cale? He's not working on Sydney's story anymore?"

"I'm working with Cale, but it's me, not him, who's working on Sydney's story."

She cleared her throat and said, "I would prefer Cale to work on the story."

I felt the heat rising to my face and I was unsure of how I should respond. "I'm sorry," I said, respectfully conceding, "I'll let him know."

I did not let Cale know, not that night at least. I did not even tell him I had talked to Martha. I thought surely there was a way I could convince her to let me do it, as though it was something I just needed to work out on my own. I seemed to think it was not choice but only my ability to convince that mattered. All the hope I felt regarding her changing her mind was a construction of my own doing. I did not take into account that she felt the way she felt and leave it at that. I was forced to go back to the knowledge, over and over, that she had, in fact, told me she wanted Cale to do it.

I went to sleep that night feeling uneasy. I had a dream in which I was asked, "Do you ever see anything other than bodies?" I had a sickening feeling when I woke up. It was not the first time I had heard those words. In my dream a man with a gun chased me. I was in a house with cold, wallpapered rooms and tall ceilings. There were beds in all the rooms, along with dressers and mirrors. In fact, all the rooms were exactly the same except for the wallpaper. I ran from room to room trying to get away from the man with the gun. I was hiding behind dressers, beds, and in one room I pulled the mirror off the wall and hid behind it. That was a mistake. He pulled the mirror away, pointed his gun at me, and asked, "Do you ever see anything other than bodies?"

The dream disturbed me that morning and I went down to Cale's office in my pajamas, knowing I would have a hard time doing any work. So I went off to the kitchen where Cale and Will were eating cereal. I told Cale what Martha had said and that I felt it might not be a good idea for me to be doing her story.

"You are the perfect person to work on her story," he responded.

"But why?" I asked. "Why am I more of a perfect person to do this story than you are? I have no experience at all. I have no idea what I'm doing!"

"If you can't find yourself, why not find Sydney?"

"What does that mean?" I asked, annoyed that I didn't really understand what he meant.

"You don't know who you are, right? He asked. So why not discover something about someone else, someone who is probably not that different from you. She's a young woman, she's about your age... maybe it will help you remember something about yourself."

For a brief fleeting moment I was filled with the hope that there was something discoverable about myself. At the same time I had the cynical thought that Cale just wanted someone to do his work for him. I knew that wasn't the case though, and even if it was, this was an opportunity, no matter how challenging of one it was.

I had to work up courage to call Martha back and ultimately decided the next time I reached out to her would be through writing. Cale seemed to be leaving it up to me to work things out with her. As I looked at the basic information about Sydney the words swam on the page. I had questions but was scared to call Martha. I wanted to inject Sydney's story into my brain like one might inject a vaccine into my arm. Or perhaps just an injection of courage would do.

If I could not do it perfectly, was there any point? I did not want to disrespect Sydney, or Martha, or anybody. I wanted it to be perfect. The stream of thoughts collided with me. I went back and forth between thinking, 'it's not going to be perfect,' and 'what if it's not perfect?'

I thought of the label of a name, the label of 'Sydney,' and wondered if writing a story was similar to naming a child. Was the story something that would always be associated with

Sydney? It only increased the pressure on me to somehow come up with the perfect story. The more I thought about it the more stressed I became. I thought of my own name, Ella, but did not know the people who had given me that name. Was it a link to the past, a beloved aunt of grandmother? Was it from popular culture, a favorite book or song? Had my mother and father given me this name lovingly? Would I ever know who they were? What if your name somehow shapes you, if you live up to, or down to, your name?

I wanted to scream. This led me to think of the invisible jar of chaos. I conjured it in my mind and unscrewed the top. I imagined it was bottomless, able to hold all the anxiety and perfectionism that might flow into it. I watched it, I would deal with it too, later, or perhaps I would let it sit until it lost its power.

Twelve

Sydney's story did not have to be perfect, it just had to be done. It had to be worked on and finished. My responsibility was doing the story, not having it be perfect. I looked at the blank notepad on Cale's desk and took the top off a pen. I decided with certainty I would wait on calling Martha back. I began to write her a letter.

Dear Martha,

I am sorry for what you and your family are going through. I know you probably have heard these words already, many times, but it is a genuine sentiment. I am so very saddened at the loss of your daughter, Sydney. I know it is Cale you want to do Sydney's story but I want you to know if I do Sydney's story I will do everything I can to honor her memory. I know I don't have the same experience Cale does, I am committed though, and I will do nothing less than my very best. I hope you will consider letting me work on her story, and again, I am truly sorry for your loss. I wish you the best in this difficult time.

Sincerely, Ella

I read and reread the letter and rewrote it once. I wished to rewrite it again. The need for perfection was still trickling into the bottomless jar, however, and I knew it was good enough. It was not perfect, but it was enough. I folded the letter carefully and put it into an envelope. I put a stamp on it and neatly printed Martha's name and address on it. I ran outside to look at the front of the de Angelo's house to find the street number, and wrote in the return address. I had planned to ask Kristen or Cale to mail it but when I went out to the front of the house the weather was unexpectedly delightful and I thought it would be nice to walk.

"I'm going to the post office," I said on my way out the door.

"Ella," Kristen said, "The post office is at least three miles away, what do you need to mail?"

"It has to do with a story I'm working on for Cale."

"You can put it in the mailbox and put the flag up," she told me. I wanted to see it going into the mail slot though.

"No, I want to get out. I'm fine, thanks." I stepped onto the front porch, knowing there was still a bit of perfection and anxiety dripping into the jar, and started walking. My walk to the post office was uneventful and enjoyable. I pulled open the heavy glass door at the post office and walked to the mail slot. I had a hard time parting with the letter. It would be up to the postal service, and then up to Martha. I let it slide in, hearing the very slight thud it made as it fell. It was an anticlimactic moment and I walked back home, uneventfully.

When I got home I decided to call Natalie. The phone was answered quickly and I asked, "Hello, may I speak to Natalie?"

"This is Natalie," she said.

"Hi, My name is Ella, I'm working on a story about Sydney Everett."

"How did you get my number?" she asked, sounding surprised.

"It was included in the notes for the story… oh, I'm writing a story about Sydney."

"What kind of story?" She asked.

"I'm working with Cale de Angelo, he's compiling stories of people who have died, just about, you know, their life, not so much about how they died. Sydney's one of the people we're doing a story on. But if you don't want to talk, I understand."

"No, no, it's ok," she said.

"Can I ask you some questions about Sydney?"

"I guess," she said with hesitation.

Then I realized this just wasn't going to work. I had no questions prepared, and I did not want this to be as uncomfortable as it was with Martha. I quickly scanned my brain for anything to ask, but came up with nothing. I thought maybe the awkwardness with Martha was there because I had talked to her over the phone. Out of nowhere I heard myself say, "I was hoping I could meet with you sometime."

"Well, maybe. What kinds of questions do you want to ask me?" She paused and said, "I don't want to talk about the accident."

"I understand," I said, hoping I sounded compassionate. "I'd love to hear from you about your relationship with Sydney and the kind of person she was."

"I'm not ready to talk about the accident," she said, forcefully this time.

"I understand," I repeated.

"Well," she said with trepidation, "I might be able to meet with you. I don't want to meet in public though. I don't want to see anybody I know."

"Really?" I said, surprised that she actually agreed. "Thank you so much Natalie. I could come to your place or you could come to mine."

"Where do you live?" she asked.

"I live in Carlton, a few miles from the Post Office, 522 Watson Drive. You're welcome to come here."

"Okay, I could do that."

"When would be good for you? Maybe a month?... I just need more time to separate myself from the accident."

We decided on a month from that Friday. And I realized it was going to be very hard to be patient.

I went into the kitchen and told Cale that Natalie had agreed to come over and let me ask her some questions. He seemed pleased with the development and said it was no problem to use his office. I decided I was glad I had a while. I had time to think.

Thirteen

Three days later I got a call from Martha. She told me she appreciated my letter but was hesitant. She said we could try though.

"I think you should talk to some of Sydney's friends for now, I had never met Natalie, but I do know some of her college and school friends," she told me.

"That would be wonderful," I responded, though I was disappointed she didn't want to talk to me. Still, things were coming together. Martha gave me the phone numbers of Sydney's friends who lived in Carlton, April, Christine, and Kalyn. April was the first one I called and it was her suggestion that we all meet together sometime. She suggested we meet at a local coffee shop. I coordinated with all of them and we decided to meet that Saturday.

Cale and I came up with prompting questions but when we all finally met I realized we needed no questions. The commonality of Sydney connected everyone, and the conversation took off quickly.

April, who had freckles and shoulder-length dark hair, and towered over all of us, went to college with Sydney. Christine, with her beautiful smile, deep Southern accent, and long brown hair, also went to college with her. Kalyn's pronounced features and gentle exterior, with her wavy auburn hair that went just past her shoulders, went to middle and high school with her. April and Christine knew each other but had only met Kalyn a few times. I felt a bit like an outsider, and enjoyed observing each of them. I did manage to wriggle in some of my prompting questions, for the sake of using what I had worked on. I asked them each how they had met Sydney, and what had drawn them to her. Kalyn, who had known Sydney the longest, had the fullest answers.

"The summer before eighth grade I moved to Carlton from Chicago," Kalyn shared. "I was completely bummed, I loved Chicago. My parents had a double mid-life crisis. My mom was 42 when she had me and my dad was 50. I have three much older siblings. I think I was a mistake baby, but neither of my parents will ever admit it. By the time I hit middle school my dad was close to retirement. My mom was an accountant for a non-profit in Chicago and was pretty burned out. The three of us had a 'family meeting,' as if we had ever had one of those before. My dad said all he wanted to do was sit in a rocking chair and drink sweet tea. By the way, he has decided he hates the sweet tea here, says it's too sweet. The next day my dad put in he was retiring and my mom put in her notice at work. They started looking for a place in North Carolina and we began packing. I didn't know anybody when I started eighth grade here. I missed Chicago and my friends there. There were so many cliques in middle school and if you were not immediately picked to be in one, you never had any chance of it. In gym class on the second day we went out to the football field to run a mile. I was athletic and a good runner but Sydney had asthma and had to stop and start. When I almost lapped her I stopped and walked beside her. I was terrified of rejection back then but made myself say hello. We walked the rest of the time and talked. She was fascinated by big cities and wanted to know all about Chicago. We went to different colleges but it's not like it's the 1900's anymore. Technology kept us constantly connected. We had a never-ending texting conversation. We never said goodbye on text because it was a four-year-long conversation. I knew I could send her a message anytime and she could send me one anytime." I smiled at her exclusion of the entire 1900's from technology.

Kalyn paused, as if to give others the chance to talk, but I could tell she wanted to continue. After waiting just a few seconds she said, "Ella, I want you to know about Sydney's character. She was rather insecure, but most people didn't realize this. She was compassionate though, and when it came down to compassionate things, she was brave. At the end of our sophomore year in high school there was a student in our grade who died in a car accident. He was a loner and neither of us knew him well. Sydney designed a huge card, made out of poster board, and went on a mission to get every single member of the sophomore class to sign it. She copied the pages from the yearbook of the whole class and checked off each person who signed it. When she had gotten all the signatures she hand-delivered it to his family, you can't mail a card that big. When she went to his house she ended up talking to his mom and stepdad for over an hour."

Kalyn's face then changed from delight to something hidden. She broke off eye contact and said, "I'm taking up all the time, I'm sorry, someone else should talk now." I sensed there was another reason she stopped talking, there seemed to be something else she wanted to say.

Neither April nor Christine had the same kind of monologue that Kalyn had, April having met her at freshman orientation in college and Christine living with her in the same dorm on the same hall their sophomore year of college. Continually, we would talk about Sydney, and then veer off into another direction, one topic leading to another. I found that Sydney had great friends, and I wanted friends like hers. At some point, I mentally crossed a line from being a researcher separate from the subject, to feeling like I had somehow slipped into Sydney's place. I did not have my own friends and here was a ready-made bunch. The three of them were all different.

April was quiet and thoughtful before she spoke. Christine seemed fun-loving and relaxed. Kalyn was a nice mix.

As I sat there watching, I wondered if Kalyn and I could be friends. She seemed a good match to me. At what point, I wondered, did one cross the line from acquaintance to friend? When we ended I did not have much of a greater amount of knowledge of Sydney but instead had a greater sense of who she was. It was something I could not put into words. Sydney's friends had given me solid information about her, but what was more important was that I had an understanding of her compassion, strength, and drive.

The de Angelos lived close to the coffee shop and I was able to walk home after we all met. I looked at the homes as I walked on the sidewalks and curbs. Each home I passed contained hundreds, thousands, or millions of memories. The people contained in the homes could look back at life and make sense of it. I could not do that. I thought about these different lives on the walk home. I was serious at times, crossing my arms and thinking about the universe, and about the hardships of life. I was playful, walking on curbs holding my arms out for balance, thinking about the wonders of the world. I was optimistic, looking ahead only, to the point I almost tripped because I refused to look down at where I was going. I was pessimistic, figuratively looking behind me, thinking of what I had lost, or imagining what I had lost. Most of all, I was me, incorporating all – the seriousness, the playfulness, the optimism, and the pessimism, into the vessel of myself.

I looked at the rectangular blocks on the sidewalk in front of me. They were uniform and laid out in mass. They were the same shape as something I had seen on the de Angelo's fridge. It was a thank you card from Kristen's cousin. It was for feeding her dogs when her cousin had gone out of town with her family. I had read and reread it, simply out of it being there right in front of me. Within that card was a mine of information. It reflected both Kristen's cousin and Kristen. It gave a glimpse into an experience Kristen had and also into the type of person she was. I wondered if there were any cards that had been given to Sydney or that Sydney had given. I had the feeling you could glimpse far into a person's life if given a stack of cards.

I was restless that night, thinking about how tempting it was to be a friend to Sydney's friends and I worried I fit in too well. I worried I had not shown enough reverence for Sydney.

I said out loud to myself, "The world does not stop turning when someone dies, no matter how much we think it should." I understood there was a person behind those words I said, a person I did not know, but who was me. I felt overwhelmed.

Fourteen

In a spur of the moment decision the next morning, I impulsively called Martha, while I had my nerve, to ask if she had any cards of Sydney's. "Martha, hi!" I said when she answered the phone, not sure where my enthusiasm was coming from. "I had a great meeting with Sydney's friends. Thank you for giving me their numbers."

"You're certainly welcome," she said. "I'm glad you all met together."

"Yes, everybody talked about how they met Sydney and experiences they had with her. Kalyn talked the most."

"Oh really, and Kalyn just talked about... Sydney?"

This struck me as an odd thing to say. "Just Sydney," I said tentatively. "Was there something else she should have talked about?"

"Oh no, not at all, just asking." Her voice had become shrill.

"Well I was calling to ask, do you have any cards that Sydney saved, that I could take a look at? Birthday cards, thank you cards, that sort of thing."

There was a pause, and then, "Yes, I do. I have a handful we found at Sydney's apartment." She paused again, as if deciding if I was worthy of looking at them. Apparently deciding so, she said, "You can stop by and pick them up if you want." Her voice was still a little shrill.

"Sure!" I said, continuing my fake confidence and ignoring the shrillness.

I told Martha I would have to let her know when I could come by. She did not live within walking distance so I was going to have to get someone to take me. My first instinct was to ask Cale, my second to ask Kristen, and my third to ask Kalyn. I decided to go with my third instinct. Kalyn was easygoing, and someone I wanted to get to know better.

Kalyn agreed right away to give me a ride and would pick me up the next evening. We stood on Martha's front porch and I knocked. A young girl came to the door, this must be

Sydney's sister, Courtney. Courtney lit up when she saw Kalyn and began to open it.

Martha came to the door next. Looking at Courtney she said, "Courtney, you know you are supposed to wait for me before opening the door."

"Mom, it's Kalyn!"

"Hi," Martha said to me through the screen door. "Hi Kalyn, I didn't realize you would be coming," she said to Kalyn. I immediately picked up on something strange and Martha became syrupy sweet at that point. "Won't you come in girls? It's so good to see you both."

"This is my daughter Courtney," Martha said to me. "Have a seat, let me grab those cards for you." I looked at Kalyn and she looked at me. The look in Kalyn's eyes was imperceptible. What was going on here? "Here you go," Martha said, sitting down across from us, with a smile on her face.

There was flat silence and I opened the top card, not sure if we were supposed to leave now or if we were supposed to make small talk. It said, *Sydney, as you wander this world don't forget where your home is. Love, Mom and Dad*

Seeing me read the card, Martha said to me, Sydney had wanderlust. She wanted to go everywhere, Europe, Australia, South America. But she was busy exploring the United States when she… when she died.

"I like that you wrote that," I said. "Home can be a center point. A place you can always go back to." Even though I did not have that center point, it was my lack of a past and home that made me know it was, in fact, important. This wisdom, I was sure, ran deeper than I could know.

"She did not, however, enjoy traveling with her family. On one trip we took she was so bored she wrote a letter to me in pig Latin. It said the car ride was the most boring thing she had ever done and she should be rewarded with a castle made of diamonds and chocolate. She must have been 11 or 12. I still have the letter." She laughed then, and I felt a barrier between us weaken. Throughout it all she looked at me and avoided Kalyn.

I smiled, again unsure if we were supposed to be staying or going. Martha did not look like she was going to say anything else, so I said, "I guess that's all I need for now. Thanks Martha."

"I hope this helps," she told me, still not looking at Kalyn. The tension between the two of them had grown during the short time we were there.

Kalyn and I walked out to the car silently. I closed the door, got in, and put on my seatbelt. Kalyn did the same. She put her key into the ignition and turned the key. She put the car into drive and as soon as we started moving I asked, "What was that about?"

"That woman," she said with exasperation, "drives me crazy."

"I could tell something wasn't right," I said.

"Courtney," she responded, "is not her daughter. She's Sydney's daughter."

"What?" I asked, with shock.

"Nobody who is not from here knows about it, as far as I know."

"I don't understand. If Courtney is Sydney's daughter why is Martha pretending like Courtney is her daughter?"

"In eleventh grade Sydney became pregnant. Sydney was pressured by her parents during her pregnancy to give up the baby for adoption, but she refused. Through many fights and more stress than any pregnant woman should undergo it was decided Martha would raise Courtney and she has always had her. I do not think it was intended to be completely kept from Courtney, but somehow, maybe because Sydney went off to college, the message never got to Courtney. It has been an unspoken rule that we do not talk to Courtney as if Sydney is her mom. Sydney's friends from college don't know she has a child."

"Why is Martha so cold to you?"

"I don't know for sure but I think it's because I know the whole story and I could break the news to Courtney, if I wanted to."

"I'm surprised she gave me your name to contact then."

"I'm a little surprised too, but I am Sydney's oldest friend, and she knows that."

"Courtney has no idea? How old is she?"

"No, she doesn't know. Courtney is nine. Sydney gave up Courtney because she was pressured to. But at the same time she believed Courtney would be better off with her parents. She believed Courtney would have a better future with them. Besides, since Courtney would be raised as her sister, she would still be in her life, just with less responsibility."

When I went home I went straight to Cale's office, and when I saw him I said, "I had an interesting time with Kalyn."

"Oh really?" he asked absentmindedly, quickly glancing up and then back at his computer.

"I learned Sydney has a daughter."

He looked at me, as if trying to ascertain if this was some kind of joke.

"Yes," I said, seeing the question in his eyes, "a daughter. I met her."

"She's old enough to *meet*?"

"You know about Sydney's sister, Courtney?" I did not wait for a response, "According to Kalyn, Courtney is not Sydney's sister, she's her daughter."

"And you believe her," he said as a statement rather than a question, he must have seen that I did.

"I do believe her, I have no reason not to. There is a 16-year age gap between Sydney and Courtney. It actually makes more sense that Courtney is her daughter, not her sister."

"This is an unexpected development," Cale said, betraying none of the surprise I knew had taken root in him.

I took the cards and went down into the cool, little used basement. It was a haven to camel crickets, but they spread away and out of my sight as I progressed downstairs. I swept the concrete floor carefully but it did not seem clean. I got two bath towels, one wet and one dry. I mopped a giant circle on the floor with the wet towel and dried it off as much as possible with the dry towel. While it dried I went and got the cards

Martha had given me. I was eager and began my project before

the floor had completely dried.

Fifteen

There were fifteen cards, what seemed to take up a tiny amount in the large basement. I read each of them as I set them down. One was not a card but a piece of computer paper with a winter scene on it. Coming from the snowman was in a talking bubble in bold marker. It said, *Carlton United Methodist Church Wishes You Good Luck On Your Exams! We Love You!*

Another card was textured with blocks of different colors making up the whole front. On the inside it said, *Sydney, Hello Dearest Friend! I thought I would just let you know how much I enjoyed spending time with you this year. We did some crazy stuff (well, mostly me, but anyway...). You are such a great, caring friend. I don't know what I'd do without you. I can't wait for more adventures next year. Thanks for being so wonderful. Love, Christine*

My favorite card was one Sydney had written to herself. On the front of the card was printed, *If this cheery little greeting adds some sunshine to your day...* and it had four cartoon flowers smiling on it. The inside finished the thought, saying, *it's because that's what we wished for.* Written by

Sydney was, *To Sydney from yourself, I know you had a rough*

day, I know you really, really wanted that job. It's not fair you

didn't get it because you would have been wonderful. It's ok to

hate that. There are things that should be hated. It's ok for you

to be angry. I am giving you a prescription for today. It's 3:09

right now. 1. Make a healthy meal (you're excessively hungry).

2. Watch a movie (a funny one). 3. Putter around for a while

(aimlessly). 4. Read (Harry Potter). 5. Pray (because it will

give you peace). 6. Go soundly (and fabulously) to sleep. Be

renewed in your sleep. Wake up and start anew. Know you can,

and will, succeed.

I loved the picture on the first one I had seen, the one

that said, *Sydney, as you wander this world don't forget where*

your home is. The front of the card looked down a long, straight

road, in a dusty desert, the sky was clear blue. As I looked at it

I thought how nice it would be for my journey to be on that

road. Instead I was on a curvy road, having no idea what was

coming up next. I picked up the cards and put the rubber band back around them. I pretended that they were mine, that there were people who loved me that much.

After looking through the cards I longed more than ever to know my roots and who I was. When I saw Cale and Kristen in the kitchen together I spontaneously interrupted their conversation, explaining that not remembering anything was hard and that I wanted to go back to the tree stump. I had completely forgotten that nobody knew anything about the tree stump and cove.

I gave them a quick version of the whole story, "Something happened right before I woke up with no memory. My wrists were bandaged." My wrists remained bandaged for part of the time I was in the hospital but they were pretty much healed and I had only worn long sleeve shirts since I had been with the de Angelos. I pushed up my sleeves and revealed purple-red scars on the inside of each wrist. I was unsure if the Social Worker had told them about this. "I think I had just gotten out of a psychiatric hospital. It's not just because of these scars I believe that, it's because something I found in the forest."

"I was walking through the forest, on a trail, trying to make my way to something, anything. I had no memory, I had no idea who I was or where I was. I came to a tree stump. It had a mug of apple cider on it. Then there was tomato soup and bread on the mug. Then I drank water from a puddle even though I did not realize I had done it until I started choking. I was thrown against a rock and the water was forced out of me. Then, on the stump, I saw a door and I opened it, it led down to a little cove that was filled with three-ring binders. There was a binder for each month of someone's life, her name is Ella. I'm Ella, I'm sure that I am Ella. I looked at the most recent binder, the one that represented me at 20-years-old. It said I was released from a psychiatric hospital, which makes this make sense," I held up my wrists. Cale and Kristen looked at me, looking like they wanted to respond but having no idea what to say.

"I'm going to go out there," I said. This was not a fact but something I wanted to do. There was no way to do this by myself. Not only did I not have a license or car but also I did not even know where the tree stump was. My statement was actually a plea for one of them to help me. There was no objection on their faces, just the visible certainty they knew I was bluffing. Cale, while I was sure he did not believe me, nonetheless said if I could find out where I had wandered out of the forest he would take me. Since I had followed a stream all the way from the stump to the road, I was sure that getting back to the place I had been picked up would work. Upon Cale telling me this I felt motivated. Whether he believed me or not he was going to take me.

Sixteen

I decided to contact the Social Worker at the hospital. Instead of calling, I wanted to go back to the hospital. It had been three weeks since I had been there, and a part of me wanted to revisit it.

I was tired of relying on people to take me everywhere. It made me feel like a child, being dependent on others for everything. Even though I was legitimately doing work for Cale, he was still doing me a favor. I was living with others, eating others' food, getting rides from other people. In a burst I wanted independence. I was 20, I was an adult and I intended to act like one. The hospital was about a 15 minute drive in the car, maybe a little less. I was going to walk there. The weather was fine, if not a little chilly, but there was no reason I couldn't walk. I took some of the money Cale had given me for helping him for lunch and set out the next morning. The walk took me nearly two hours. I left at 9:00 and got there at almost 10:45. As I walked on the side of the highway, on sidewalks, crossing streets, I kept thinking how I hoped the Social Worker was there, I had gone a long way and I didn't want it to be for nothing. By the time I got there I was in a pretty bad mood, mostly because I had become quite hungry as I walked. I walked into the front, automatic doors of the hospital and went to the front desk.

"Hi," I said to the woman sitting behind the front desk. "I'm looking for the Social Worker."

"What's the name?"

"Oh, Mark, Mike, something with an M. Something like that." I hoped that was enough information.

"Marcus Johnson?" she questioned.

"Yes! That's it! His name was Marcus."

"Office 102B" she told me. "Just take a right at the gift shop, it's in that direction."

"Thank you!" I said, forgetting about my hunger. I went toward the gift shop and to the right, almost in a skip. The office was easy to find and just before I went into the office I said a quick prayer that he would be in there. I looked in and there he was, sitting at the desk, just sitting, right in front of me. My face broke out into a huge smile.

"Hi, Marcus."

"Hi Ella!"

"I'm so glad to see you. How are you doing?" I asked.

"I'm just fine, how have you adjusted to living with the de Angelos?"

"It's ok," I said, "I'm eager to be more independent, but they're good people."

"I understand. One step at a time!" his cheerful disposition had not dissipated, but this time I appreciated it, I had started at some point to see him as an ally rather than an adversary.

"I have a question for you," I told him.

"Sure, would you like to sit down?"

"Thanks," I said, sitting into one of the comfortable looking chairs.

"I want to go back out to where I was found, the place in the road I collapsed. Can you tell me where that is?"

"Oh sure, yes, probably. I don't know offhand but can try to find out."

"That would be amazing," I said. "It's just, I want to see the place, see if I can remember anything." That was close enough to the truth, I supposed.

"Ella, I'll look into it and let you know. Can I reach you at the de Angelos'?"

"Yes, that would be fine."

"Really, Ella, how are you doing?"

"Oh, well, okay," I said, and could hear the truth that I was barely okay leaking out of my voice. "Not great," I said, probably unnecessarily, this truth that had been in the margins had probably been evident.

"How's your memory coming?"

"It's not." I said, without going into detail, and then, "I'm hoping being out there in the woods might help me remember something."

"How's the family?" he asked, with concern.

"They're fine," I said slowly, as if it was a phrase I was not so sure about.

"But you're still having a hard time? Tell me about it."

Was this therapy? I thought to myself. Social Workers weren't therapists, were they? I panicked for a moment and then got over it and decided to simply answer the question.

"Well, yeah, I want to be more independent. I am an adult and I feel like I am living a child's life. Cale is paying me to help him with his stories, but it's not a real job. I want a job, and a car, and my own place to live. I want to be an adult. I am an adult so I want to be, you know, adult-like."

"Of course," he said, "Of course you do. You will get there. Remember, one step at a time."

"What should I do?" I asked, knowing that it was a broad question, but feeling that I had a broad problem. I was surprised at myself for soliciting his opinion.

"If you're taking it one step at a time, what step do you feel would be good for you to take?"

"I'd like to get a job," I told him.

"That's an excellent first step," he said.

"Actually, I'd like to get a job I could walk to," I don't want to keep relying on others for rides. The de Angelos live right in town, so I think that's doable. I am willing to walk. I walked here today."

"Good for you, and how long did that take you?"

"I don't know exactly, a little under two hours."

"You are to be commended for your determination," he said.

"Thank you," I responded, feeling a small swell of pride, and the tiniest bit vexed by what seemed like unjustified praise.

"Have you been looking for any jobs near the de Angelo's?"

"No," I said, shocked that indeed, I hadn't. "I plan to soon though. I will… seeing you is giving me a little push. I have wanted to but at the same time I have been scared. What if I can't do it?"

"Ella, there's no need to see it as all or nothing. There might be things you struggle with, but that doesn't mean you can't do anything. You are ready to take the next step, and I encourage you to do just that. Actually, I know it's a long walk, but you might want to look at a job here at the hospital." I felt my eyes brighten and my face flush, that was a great idea! It was a long walk, but my immediate excitement at the suggestion made me think he was on to something.

"Do you know of any jobs that are open?" I asked.

"No, Ella, but you can look on our website." I wanted to look right that moment. I did not want to wait a second longer. I took a deep breath and calmed myself.

"Yes," I said with a façade of calm, "I will do that." I felt my legs begin moving, a slight pumping up and down, as if had too much caffeine. I was at a new level of motivation. "Thank you, Marcus," I said, feeling guilty that I had thought badly of him before.

"You're welcome Ella, I will see if I can find out the place where you were picked up and I will be in touch."

I stood up and held up my hand to shake his, it felt a little odd, like it was a forgotten habit, but it felt right at the same time. We shook hands and I turned and walked out. I felt that I had ascended a level, some level, like I was not in the same place I had been when I walked in.

I had forgotten my hunger, but I felt a wave of dizziness and decided it was time to find some food. I considered the hospital cafeteria, but I had seen a small restaurant across the street and not far down from the hospital. I walked there slowly, daydreaming about my future. *'Jennifer's Restaurant,'* it said. I walked in and saw a sign to seat myself. It was half full and I saw an open booth. I went and sat down and a server brought me a menu and a hearty welcome.

"Hi!" I said, thinking I was probably going to come off as cheerful as the Social Worker.

"What would you like to drink?" she asked me.

I looked down at the menu. It said breakfast was served all day long and I decided to go with breakfast. That meant coffee. I ordered the coffee and she walked off. I checked in my pocket to make sure my money was there. I had a ten-dollar bill.

I chose a breakfast burrito when she brought my coffee and a handful of sugar and cream I asked her how the breakfast burritos were.

"My favorite!" she said.

"That's what I'll have," I told her. Then, an afterthought I asked, "Are you hiring?"

"I'm not sure, but I can give you an application."

"Sure! Thank you."

She walked to the counter and then turned back toward me with an application. I set it squarely in front of me and then pushed it aside to put cream and an excessive amount of sugar in my coffee. I saw no reason not to fill it out right at that moment and walked up to the counter and asked for a pen.

I thought it odd that I had not noticed my last name in the binders, and wondered if it had been in there. Surely that would have made it easier to figure out who I was.

I looked around the room, trying to come up with a last name. I could come up with nothing so I put down 'Ella de Angelo,' slightly annoyed at this lack of personal identity. I was filling in my address and such when my breakfast burrito came. I carefully pushed the application to the far end of the table and suddenly became even hungrier.

"Thank you," I told her, and I began to eat. The tortilla was filled with eggs, sausage and cheese and there were home fries on the side. After I had eaten almost all of the delicious food I became full as suddenly as I my wave of hunger had come. I drank a sip of the coffee, which had become lukewarm. I pushed the plate away, ready to finish the application. Wanting it to be in pristine condition I went to wash my hands. I went into the apple-scented bathroom and washed and dried my hands. When I came out the server asked if I wanted more coffee.

"That would be lovely," I told her, thinking that was an oddly proper thing for me to say, but that it would, in fact, be lovely. I added cream again and loads of sugar, wiped the spot in front of me with a napkin, and pulled the application back to me."

The application asked for previous jobs and references and I did not know what to put.

I put 'Writer and Editor' down as a job, thinking that sounded official. For references, I put down Marcus Johnson and Cale de Angelo. I looked up the number for the hospital in the restaurant's phone book to put with Marcus's name. When I finished I drank a few more sips of my coffee and then went to the cash register, with my ticket and application. I handed the server my application and she said she would give it to the manager. Then I gave her my ticket. I paid with the ten-dollar bill and left the money she returned to me on the table.

As I began my walk back home I felt accomplished and satisfied. I walked back the same way I had come and thought about how if I worked at the hospital or Jennifer's Restaurant that would mean an almost four-hour round trip if I insisted on walking every time, and winter was approaching. The walk teetered between a head full of thoughts and being boring.

When I got back I did not know what to do with myself. I had a strong desire to tell someone I was on my next step.

When I walked into the kitchen Kristen told me that Marcus Johnson from the hospital had called for me. I thought about how impressively fast that had happened and I called back immediately. It went to his voicemail and that was something I could barely stand, I was so eager to know. I left a message and then went into Cale's office to look up jobs at the hospital, but I couldn't focus. When I heard the phone ring I quickly and loudly stated, with my continuing façade of calm, "I'll get it." I picked up the phone and it was Marcus.

"Ella, it turned out to be very easy. The name of the woman who picked you up was in your file and I called her. She did not know where exactly she picked you up but she said it was just past mile marker 127 coming from town."

"Thank you, Marcus! Oh, and I applied for a job at Jennifer's Restaurant and put you down as a reference. Is that ok?"

"Sure thing. Let me know if you need anything else, Ella. Good luck."

I went straight to Cale and told him I had found the place and asked if he could still take me. Cale told me he could not take me for a few days, but yes, he would take me.

Seventeen

A few days later Cale and I set out for mile marker 127. It took a little searching, but we found the stream and followed it in for about half an hour. Where the stream converged with the trail I had been on, the stump was right there in front of us. It all went more smoothly than I had expected. The stump was right in front of my eyes as well as the rock. The little dip of land that had puddled before was there too, dry now. The stump had no apple cider on it, or tomato soup, or bread, and it certainly had no door in it.

I went and leaned against the tall, flat rock. I closed my eyes, pushed away from the rock, and screamed.

"Ella!" Cale said, after I stopped, and sounding worried, "Why are you screaming?"

I smiled and leaned back against the rock. "When I woke up with no memory one of the things I did was scream. I was in a big field and nothing was familiar. I felt compelled to scream, maybe out of frustration. After I screamed it felt so good I decided to scream again." Concerned this might sound a little strange, as an afterthought, I added, "Also, I thought it might attract anyone who was around."

I looked at the rock. There was a slightly winding line running down the rock that had not been there before. It was an indention that was barely visible. I ran my finger from the top of the line all the way down to the bottom. "Look, Cale," I said, "Look at this line." Cale came over and ran his finger down it. Suddenly a line of water began running slowly down the rock in the indent of the line.

"What is happening?" Cale asked, taking his finger away from the rock. The line sank deeper into the rock and the flow of water increased. Then, like a true waterfall, the water flowed over the whole rock. I started laughing and Cale just stared. I cupped my hands and juxtaposed them with the rock. I drank the water that pooled in my hands, drops of water hitting my arms and face. Cale took a deep sigh and crossed his arms.

"Cale, what's wrong?"

Cale looked away from the rock and at me, "This is not right, is this actually happening? It can't be, can it?"

"It's definitely happening, this is a special place. I see what's happening too."

"Right, so we're both seeing things," he responded.

"Think what you want," I said, "I told you this was not a normal place."

"I thought that was your head injury talking," he said.

"Cale! You know there was no evidence of a head injury."

"Why can't you remember anything then? Something must have happened."

"It wasn't a head injury, Cale, that has been determined."

Out of my periphery view I could tell that the water had changed. I turned and looked and saw it was no longer water that flowed down the rock. It was crimson, it was wine. It no longer flowed onto the ground, instead it was flowing into what appeared to be a large, invisible, bowl. Just as quickly as it started, it stopped, the bowl of wine full. With the wine, I would have to agree with Cale that it was all a little bizarre, but

I could not concede that to Cale. He was already a mess on his own, moving to sit on the stump, as though it was so much to take in he could no longer stand. I looked at Cale sitting on the stump and saw the outline of a door as well as hinges and a handle.

"Cale! The stump!"

Cale looked down and said, "Ella, this makes no sense at all." He stood up, looking down at the door and I grabbed the handle and pulled, opening the door. I looked down, expecting to see stairs but instead saw a picnic basket.

I pulled out the heavy, wicker picnic basket. I closed the door and set the picnic basket on top. I opened the basket and two ceramic wine glasses sat on top. I went over and dipped each glass into the wine, carrying them back over to the stump. Next in the basket were apples, cheese, and homemade bread. There were two beautiful ceramic plates that matched the glasses, a knife, and cloth napkins.

"Cale, I know you think this is all crazy but somehow I know it makes sense. The food is safe and it looks great. We used the stump as both our table and our cutting board. I started out with a thick slice and instinctively I dipped it into the wine. Hope surged in me then, and I knew this was right. I felt peaceful, it was the same feeling I had when I dipped the tomato soup into the bread. We both ate. I ate slices of apple with slices of cheese and another slice of bread dipped in wine. I drank all the wine in my glass and then refilled it. I finished my second glass of wine quickly and then wanted to laugh at nothing and say anything. I started to talk. We sat there, and I talked. My words circumvented my mind and went out my mouth.

"When I was growing up," I heard myself say, "My grandfather brought liquor every Thanksgiving for the adults. He even brought a folding table he set up. When I was ten and nobody was near the table, I poured a long, clear stream of vodka into my Sprite. I fell asleep before we even had dinner."

"Ella, you just remembered something about your past," Cale said, and I focused then. I could see the table clearly. There was a green tablecloth, an ice bucket, the forbidden bottles of liquor, and the bowl of salty, crunchy peanuts. I did not remember my grandfather but I knew the set up was his.

"How did I remember that? Was that a real memory?"

"Ella, I don't know how anything is happening out here." I got another glass of wine and sat back down. I tore off a small piece of bread and dipped it into the wine, cupping my hand under it to keep it from dripping on the ground. I did not understand why I would do that, as it would not matter if it dripped onto the ground, but it felt like an automatic motion.

I put everything in the picnic basket and put it at the base of the stump. I opened the door again, without expectation. The steps were there and my heart thrilled.

"Come down with me," I said. I walked down the steps slowly, thinking I had drunk too much wine. I wondered if there would be enough room for two people. It had been pretty tight with just me. Cale was right behind me and by the time we were there down there I saw there was plenty of room. Had I misjudged the space or had it gotten bigger?

"I can't believe this," Cale said.

"Cale, all these binders are about who I am. We will be able to find out more about me than either of us ever wanted to know."

Cale picked up a binder on the top of one of the stacks. As he flipped through it he said, Ella, there's no way we can go through all of these. Let's take some of the binders back with us."

It had not occurred to me that I could take something out of the cove, but it made sense. We took a binder from within every fourth stack. When we walked out of the cove I grabbed the picnic basket and put it in the cove. I closed the door to the cove and saw the outline seal shut, as if it had not been there at all. We walked back to the car in fading light.

After getting home I took the binders to the living room and sat on the floor. I browsed through all of them and then ate dinner with the family. After dinner I browsed through all of them again and then took them and left them in Cale's office. Then I went to my bedroom, took off my jeans, and crawled into bed. I lay restless, until I finally got up in the early hours of the morning, put my jeans back on, and crept downstairs, going into Cale's office. I opened the most recent binder, the one at 20 years. There was the usual block of colored lines and the 21st line down was bold. I knew that line was bold because I was 20, because that was the 21st year of my life. I looked at the binders to make sure my deduction about the colored lines was right. At age four the fifth line was bold, at age eight the ninth line, at age twelve the thirteenth line, and at age 16 the seventeenth line. I opened the age 20 binder and counted down again, it was definitely 21 lines down. Then I counted the rest of the way down. There were 90 lines total. Did that mean I would die at 89?

The next page had a picture of Ella, a young woman who I knew was me, it only took a mirror to prove that. I went through the 21st year binder page by page. The third page, after the block of colored lines on the first page, and the picture on the second page, was titled, 'Monthly Overview.'

The monthly overview said, '*Ella had a very mixed month. It was filled with the good and bad of life on Earth. She was born in this month 20 years ago. There was joy on her birthday and she and her loved ones celebrated. The first two weeks of the month were filled with work and play and her weekends were filled with breakfast outings, window-shopping, and relaxation. The third week of the month she found out Corey had died and memories from many years ago began to come back to her. She began to become depressed. She unearthed the necklace Corey had given her, wondering why she had kept it all that time, she couldn't seem to let it go, although she wanted to leave Corey behind completely.'*

The following thirty pages each represented one day of the month, and I went through them carefully. Page six was titled, '*September 3rd*,' this page said, '*Ella turned 20 today. She went to dinner and celebrated with her friends. She proclaimed that 20 was the oldest she had ever been and was introspective. She was excited about the future and she had feelings of awe at the possibilities that existed. Her day began early and she took her time to look nice. Jacob sent her flowers at work, roses and chrysanthemums. At the restaurant that night she insisted the wait staff not know about her birthday,*

she did not want to be sung to. It seemed she went to bed

feeling loved and excited for the next year of her life.'

Page 24 was titled, '*September 26.*' September 26 said,

'*Today was a perfect storm of distress for Ella. Her depression*

had been deepening since she heard about Corey dying.

Everything that had once hurt her about Corey came back. It

changed her reality. She began to lose touch with who she was

as she was immersed in the way she had once been so

destroyed by a single act. She became guarded and internal

and very vulnerable. She was filled with regret and grief and

wondered if it was because of her that Corey died. In a moment

of panic, feeling things she had not felt in years, she closed her

eyes and slashed her wrists, desperate for the turmoil and pain

to go away. In another moment of panic, she called 911,

regretting what she had done, not understanding what she had

done. She was still greatly distressed and was admitted to a

psychiatric hospital.'

I glanced at the next pages as the darkness of night crept toward morning. On September 27, '*...the hospital was a new world, Ella was scared and ashamed...*' On September 28, '*...she learned new ways to cope with her pain...*' on September 29, '*...she offers forgiveness to herself and at the same time knows there is nothing to forgive herself for...*' On September 30, '*...Ella continues to feel ashamed, and she is also angry. She wants to leave the hospital and at the same time is scared to leave...*'

The remaining pages held a variety of information. Page 34 was labeled, '*Struggles,*' and listed on its page things that had been hard that month. Page 35 was labeled, '*Triumphs,*' outlining what had been achieved that month. Page 26 was labeled, '*Illness,*' and told of physical and mental health problems. '*...Ella primarily struggled with mental health...*' Page 37 was labeled, '*Health,*' and described ways in which health was thriving. '*...She coped as well as she knew how to...*' Page 38 was labeled, '*Finances,*' and gave an overview of her financial situation. '*...Having health insurance was her* saving grace…' Page 39 was labeled, '*Fulfillment of Needs,*' and told of what had been needed that month, emotionally, and how those needs were met. '*…From the outside looking in Ella seems to have everything she needs, and many things she wants. This is only true for material possessions…*' Page 40 was labeled, '*Given,*' and showed ways in which she had shown generosity. '*..She gave of herself to other patients…*' Page 41 was labeled, '*Taken*' and held ways in which others had been generous. Page 42 was labeled, '*Resolved*' and gave ways things had been resolved. '*…She now knows Corey can never hurt her or anyone else again...*' Page 43 was labeled, '*Carry Over,*' and listed issues that would be carried over to the next month. '*…Her feelings of shame will need more time to resolve...*' Page 44 and 45 were a two-page spread, labeled, '*Core Impacts,*' telling a basic overview of everything. '*…Ella is not completely undamaged, but she's also resilient. There is no question her impact on the world is important. It is time to begin healing from something she would not let herself feel for many years...*' Taped to the back inside cover was a necklace.

Eighteen

I took the tape off and held the necklace by its chain. The necklace looked cheap. It was gold colored, but I did not think it was real gold. On its chain was a small heart. The chain was long and I slipped it over my head and grasped the heart in my hand. For just a moment I seemed to remember everything and at the same time my energy dropped to the floor. The remembrance happened so fast I hardly retained any of it. The question from my dreams, 'Do you ever see anything other than bodies?' came back to me, and stayed with me. I saw myself as a young girl, about the same age as Hazel and Courtney. I saw a boy handing me the necklace. He was older than I was and I had no recollection of him. I held the heart tightly and then put it on.

I closed the binder and went back upstairs, again taking off my jeans and sliding into bed. This time I fell to sleep very shortly after closing my eyes. I woke up after a couple of hours, feeling unrested. It was Sunday morning and there was a bustle in the house, everybody was getting ready to go to church. I had been to church with them before, but enjoyed the peace at home for a couple of hours with nobody there but me. After they left, I went to the kitchen and assembled graham crackers topped with peanut butter and banana slices. I made hot chocolate and sat in front of the television. I turned it on and the channel it showed a mega church service. I left it there and watched absentmindedly while I ate. But the church service sank into my head and I wondered about God. Then I remembered something. I remembered someone teaching me about God. I could not remember much, it was mostly a feeling, and I knew it was an old feeling. I knew it was from long before I lost my memory.

After the night of looking through the binder, after I ate the graham crackers with peanut butter and banana, after the church service, and after I wondered about God, I went into the bathroom and looked into the mirror at the heart that lay on my chest. I knew there was a time before when I had laid it on my chest, just as it did now. I decided to keep it on, it was the only tangible link to the past I had.

Beginning that morning, depression began to ravage me. It caught me by surprise and changed my outlook on life. It seemed to color everything. For the two weeks after that morning I was only happy in small increments, usually when I was lost in the binders, or Sydney's story, or a conversation with Cale or Kalyn. Like I had done with the chaos, I wanted to seal my good moods in an invisible jar and set it on a shelf. I wanted to be able to store them so when the proverbial emotional hunger hit and I was in need of nourishment I would have them right there. I could fill them with contentment, excitement, peace, happiness, and so on. I found that when depression is almost always attacking you, it's hard to collect big stores of these things. During this time I clung to a poem I had found in the binder, one I had written in the hospital.

Give me mountainscapes

Oceans to swim

Sunshine that sparkles

Flowers to pick

Fields of endlessness

But first, people to love

In my mind, I added to it:

Give me mountainscapes – beauty

Oceans to swim – freedom

Sunshine that sparkles – warmth

Flowers to pick – color

Fields of endlessness – wonder

But first, people to love…

There was a comfort I felt in that poem in those times depression ravaged me. When everything seemed heavy, it brought lightness. It represented something essential I wanted in my life. I wanted beauty, freedom, warmth, color, and wonder. First and foremost though, I needed people. From the beginning of waking up in the field, it had been other people I yearned for. In deep depression it was a wonderful though to wish for.

My sleep had been greatly disrupted, and my nights became mostly sleepless. My sadness was usually not sharp, but it was constant. At those times I held the heart in my hand, sadness seemed to take me over. It was when I was caught in hopelessness, and everything was quiet that I thought about God. I wondered what God was doing at the moment. Was God judging me? Did he resent me by knowing despite all I had, I was still not happy? Sleep was threadbare, I seemed to be always awake. My thoughts became bizarre and paranoid on those nights I did not sleep, as I held the heart in my hand. I did not seem to break from the spell until I reached a point of complete exhaustion. That point was when I let go of the tight grip I had on the heart. Letting it rest, my body also rested. I would reach a point of acceptance of my struggle. When that happened things seemed to get a bit easier. This acceptance made me stop fighting, and helped me relax.

Although my nights were mostly sleepless, on nights I did sleep I often had variations of the dream where someone said to me, 'Do you ever see anything other than bodies?' I had a dream like that almost every night I was able to get some sleep.

One Friday night I went to bed at 11:00 and finally fell asleep the next morning about 7:00. I got out of bed at 9:00 and went into the kitchen, remembering Hazel had soccer games on Saturday mornings. If the pattern held true, I was sure Will was still asleep. I poured Lucky Charms and milk into a bowl. I walked around the house, carrying the bowl in my hand and slowly eating the cereal and slurping milk.

As I walked around the house I peered into the picture frames. There were vacation photos, school photos, portrait photos, and photos of past generations. I finished my cereal and put the bowl down on the coffee table. As I set it down I started to feel like I was not actually in my body. I had a feeling of unbearable heaviness at my core. Perhaps this thing in me, this thing that was destroying my thoughts and making me so very sad was not an intrinsic part of me. Perhaps it was more like something I carried.

I was only beginning to get back memories and feelings and during this time I wanted to weed out the bad things. It was at the conception of remembering how this depression had been brought on. It had something to do with Corey and something to do with the necklace. I became determined to figure out how to resolve what was, for then, right at the surface.

I picked up my cereal bowl and carried it to the kitchen. I washed the bowl. I still felt on the outside of myself though. I thought of how liberated I felt the previous times I screamed. Without making a conscious decision to do so, I began to scream.

Swiftly Will was there, "What's wrong?" he asked, looking genuinely concerned. I appreciated his earnestness.

"I'm sorry Will, there is nothing to worry about. I hope I didn't wake you up."

"But you were screaming," he said.

"I know, sometimes when I get frustrated I scream." He looked at me with deadpan eyes as if to say, 'you have got to be kidding me.'

"Ok," he said, "whatever you say." He shook his head and turned around. "I'm going back to sleep."

"Sorry again," I called as he walked away.

When Cale, Kristen, and Hazel got home I was in the kitchen, cleaning. As I washed the dishes I thought about the way I had felt outside of myself, and how the screaming helped reverse that. After a few minutes Cale came into the kitchen.

"Ella," he said, "Will tells me you were screaming in the house this morning. He's worried. I know you did this out in the woods, and it seemed like something you did when you were frustrated. What's going on?" As Cale finished his question Kristen walked in.

"Yes, what's going on?" she repeated. They asked the same question, but in very different manners. I wanted to leave, to run down the street, away from everything.

Looking at neither of them, I said, "It was just, I felt outside of myself. Like I wasn't me. In the past, when I have screamed, it seemed to calm me."

"And did it calm you this time?" Kristen asked.

"Actually, yes, it did."

I did not completely understand why it was that screaming helped me, but I knew it was a release, and I knew it centered me. It was as if one by one things had built up in me, my depression, disturbing dreams, inability to sleep, and that what those photos I had been looking at that morning ultimately did was make me feel like an outsider. Each time there was more added to me, like I was a cup being filled with water. Sometimes it only takes a drop more for water to start sliding down the sides. The pictures of their happy family were that drop. When the water started sliding down, that was when I felt the urge to scream. Screaming soaked up the excess water, I was still filled to the brim, but as long as it was contained, it was bearable.

Something I had discovered about myself was when I tried something new, often I eventually grew into it and it did fit me. For example, when Kristen painted my fingernails pink the first week I was there, it did not fit who I was. It was an admirable attempt to reach out to me. It had two coats and a top coat, it stayed on for over a week and I eventually got used to it, even started to like it.

I was a blank slate, a bare wall. Everything added to it. In another admirable move Kristen brought me clothes, but I did not like them much. I got used to them too, and even started to like them. I was a jumble and seemed to have little identity of my own.

It was a similar experience with Sydney's friends. Unlike the nail polish and clothes, they had a positive effect on me from the beginning. As time went by though, they fit as my friends and not only Sydney's friends. I had a little bit of anxiousness that the only friends I had were actually Sydney's friends, but my need for friends overrode that anxiousness.

I was committed to Sydney's story, even though there was a great deal going on in my mind. I called them each, to meet again, telling them I wanted to jump into Sydney's story. It was not purely because of that. Not even close if I was honest. I seemed to be trapped in depression and my sleepless nights were incredibly isolating. I hoped meeting again would help me escape these things. Focusing on something different, I thought, would help, and it proved that it did. It also gave me time to be lost in joy, to be involved in something other than

my own mind.

Nineteen

When I first met Cale and Kristen, Martha, and
Sydney's friends, when I first met anyone, I found myself
inadvertently and automatically judging them. Not being
judgmental in a critical way, just judging who a person was, so
I could get a hold of them. I would see a face initially, once
really, and every time after that it was the person. Those people
I came to know, if they were to become more beautiful or less
so by the standards of society, I would see they looked
different, but only that. I would always notice the way a person
looked, but primarily I saw what was not the exterior.

When I saw Kalyn, April, and Christine that particular
time was when I realized this. They were a lovely set of young
women, but that was incidental, maybe making life easier for
them in some ways and harder in others. That day we met
Christine came in with a blond pixie haircut. She had been a
long-hair brunette the last time I saw her. It took a minute for
me to adjust, but I saw in her eyes she was not her shell. Her
deeper, permanent, unchanging beauty was inside.

That day, when I met Sydney's friends… my friends… at the coffee shop, I was very comfortable. My earlier anxiety about hijacking Sydney's friends was still there, but had diminished. I had connected with each of them on a different level. It was Kalyn I connected with the most. There was not a set topic for the meeting. My reason for calling them was my need for connection. I think at least Kalyn knew this to some degree. Meeting ended up being a good thing because it was on that day Kalyn told April and Christine about Courtney. It was not a topic that was planned. We were all there, seated with our drinks. I had a cup of house coffee, cream and sugar. We talked about minor things, like the weather and Christine's blond pixie cut and whether we would ever have the nerve to chop off all our hair.

Out of the blue, Kalyn took the floor, as if the inconsequential topics we were discussing were unsatisfying to her. "Did either of you, April or Christine, know Sydney had a child when she was in high school?" I looked at April and Christine. April's eyebrows were raised and Christine's face was blank. Neither of them knew anything about this. Having met Sydney in college, they had not witnessed an expanding belly of pregnancy. Kalyn told them about how Sydney's parents were raising Courtney, and that she had been raised as Sydney's sister. She told them how much Sydney loved Courtney, and how she had wanted to give Courtney the best life possible.

April and Christine were surprised but took this news in stride. The conversation from there was free form, comfortable, and very much a celebration of Sydney. It was clear Sydney lived her life in a way that when she was gone, you could take a deep breath, sigh, and feel satisfied she had squeezed every drop of who she was in the world. That day there was a new energy between us.

This good time emboldened me, it was a short respite from my depression, and I felt the motivation to continue on with the discovery of my past and myself. I had looked through the other binders Cale and I had brought back with us. They were interesting, but did not provide anything groundbreaking. I still wore the necklace.

After April and Christine left, Kalyn and I lingered at the coffee shop. I felt sadness creep back into my veins, without such a major distraction, but it didn't come all the way back in, Kalyn was still there. I felt inspired by the way Kalyn had told about Courtney with no warning and I attempted to do the same. I gave a preface of, "You're probably going to think I'm crazy." Then I told her about waking up in the field, the tree stump and cove, the apple cider, the tomato soup and bread, the hospital, the binders, and the depression. It was a relief to get this all out, but I wondered if I had said too much.

Kalyn listened intently and though I believed nobody would believe my story outright, she seemed to be giving me the benefit of the doubt. It was easy to see a person and not break the surface. I knew on the surface Kalyn would never guess all these things I told her and I was okay with that. While I did not want to be alone in my story it was not necessary that everybody knew. It felt like I was giving Kalyn something precious and by doing so I was saying, 'I trust you.' I hoped Kalyn and whoever else came along would accept that broken, scratched, worn, and sparkling piece of me.

"I don't know what to say," she said, "but it's one of the most interesting stories I have ever heard. I'm glad you told me, I'm just not sure what to make of it. It must be difficult to have lost your memory."

"It is hard," I said, latching onto her understanding. "Other than a few scattered memories the only thing I know about who I am is what I have seen in the binders." Hesitating, and not having planned on this, I said, "That leads me to a question I have."

"Oh," Kalyn said, not expecting something else.

I went for it, "I have no driver's license that I know of, and even if I did, I don't have a car. I want to go back and exchange the binders I have for new ones. Do you think you might be willing to take me to the cove at some point?"

"Yes," she said, right away, "I would love to, I'm really curious." We decided to go the next day because she did not have to go into work until evening.

The rest of the day passed very slowly and I was up with the sun the next morning. Kalyn picked me up at 9:00 and we headed out. When we reached the spot where Cale and I had stopped we got out of the car and began to walk, following the stream. I had a camera with me, this time I would take pictures. My anticipation was great and I was excited for Kalyn to see the cove. We reached the stump and it looked very ordinary, again. The stump showed no signs of a door and the rock was dry. I was not worried, I was sure it would open. We sat and talked but after an hour had passed nothing had happened.

"I don't know what to do!" I exclaimed, "Last time it opened with no problem." We continued to sit on the stump and wait. I went back and forth between the rock and the stump, literally, I thought to myself, I was between a rock and a hard place. We alternated between silence and mindless chatter. After another hour passed we gave up. As we walked back to the car I said, "I promise you Kalyn, I'm not making this up. Please believe me."

"I do believe you," she said, "Maybe we can try another time."

The car ride home was quiet and when we got there I put on a brave face. "I'm sorry it was a waste of time, I will try to figure out what happened." I acted optimistic but I was devastated. I repeated, "What happened?" over and over as I walked from the driveway to the front door.

When I reached the front door the fact that the driveway was empty hit me. No one was home. In that moment, the inside of an empty house seemed like a coffin. I decided to go to the back yard. There was a play set Hazel had grown out of, a small pool, and sidewalk chalk.

I picked up the bucket of chalk and took it over by the pool. I sat on the concrete and started drawing colorful designs with the chalk. After drawing for a while I heard a car door slam. After a few minutes I stood up, looking down at what I had done. In the mass of color the design that clearly stood out was a rainbow. I went into the house. It was Will and his girlfriend. I made distracted conversation. As we talked I looked at my chalk covered hands. They looked dusty and dry. I flashed back to many years before and made a connection to the past. In that rainbow was a truth. My spirits lifted. Rainbows had something to do with God. I remembered hearing a story. I remembered lying in bed and someone reading me a story. The story had a rainbow. I had the feeling that a rainbow represented something good.

Then a memory came. I was small, five or six years old. I was lying on my back on a hammock and I was looking at a rainbow. It was a beautiful, brilliant rainbow. The rope hammock was wet and the ropes made my clothes wet in a criss -ross pattern. I had a banana popsicle in my hand and I was happy to my core.

I must have paused during my remembrance. When I refocused on Will and his girlfriend they were looking at me as though waiting for me to say something. I had been in the middle of conversation when the memory came.

"I've just been playing around with the chalk," I said, knowing that was probably not what we had been talking about. "I think I will go back out there." I opened the sliding glass door and stepped out, closing it behind me. I looked at the rainbow again and saw scattered nubs of chalk everywhere. I wiped my chalk-encrusted hands on my black shirt. The sky was cloudy but the afternoon sun still poured on me. I lay on my back, on my chalk creation. When I woke it was dark. I could feel the slightest sunburn on my face and arms. I went inside, not totally sure if it was night or morning. Dinner was being cooked, it was spaghetti night.

After a muttered hello to Kristen, the only way I seemed capable to talking immediately after waking up, I went upstairs to my bedroom. I looked in the mirror and my skin definitely had a pink tint to it. I felt unpleasant and hot and decided to take a cool shower. I got out, towel drying my hair and then pulling it into a ponytail. I put on comfortable sweatpants and a long sleeve t-shirt. I went downstairs and they had already started eating. I watched them at the table, talking and engaged. "Maybe one day I will have a real family too," I whispered.

I was still disheartened by the morning's failure at the cove and when Cale asked me about it after dinner I made an excuse and said I would tell him later. I was unusually avoidant and picked out a book I found on one of Cale's overcrowded bookshelves. I went to my room, started to read, and then drifted into a fitful sleep. I woke before everybody else in the morning. I was sitting in Cale's office scanning the world news on the Internet when I heard coffee being prepared. I went into the kitchen and saw Cale yawning.

"I'm ready to talk, Cale, if you have a few minutes."

"Shoot," he said sleepily. I sat down at the kitchen table.

"Cale, I don't know what happened. The stump didn't open, the rock was dry, there was no picnic, and there was no cove. There was nothing!"

"Who knows what makes that stump open. Maybe it's just chance. You can always try again."

"I intend to try again," I said, unnecessarily defensive, "But I would like some sort of guarantee it will open before dragging someone out there." I drifted to the day, wondering about Jennifer's Restaurant. I had no energy and mostly lay in bed and read. I didn't know when I would snap out of the never-ending bad mood.

Twenty

The night came slowly, and I had regret that I had accomplished nothing that day. But that night I had a strange dream. I was watching two fish in a bowl. There was a castle in the middle of the bowl. The two fish were circling around it, going in opposite directions. One fish was green and the other one was blue. The castle had an arched door that was big enough for the fish to enter simultaneously from either side and swim to the opposite sides of the bowl. The fish slowed to a stop and were on either side of the castle. Both fish then swam through the door of the castle at the same time, passing each other.

Upon passing through both fish began circling again. Soon the blue fish's behavior changed. The blue fish swam fast and aggressively. The green fish continued to swim gracefully. Then, after a few moments, when they were on either side of the castle again, both fish swam through the castle door. The green fish swam through the door as it had before. The blue fish swam through, but there seemed to be some resistance. The blue fish did not go through as easily as the green fish had. The two fish began circling again. The blue fish swam faster, more aggressively, this time slamming into the green fish's side when it passed it. The green fish continued to swim gracefully. Again, at a point when they were on either side of the castle, they both swam toward the door. The green fish swam through but the blue fish seemed to slam into an invisible barrier, it was unable to go through. I woke up and looked at the clock, it was 2:22 in the morning. I lay on my side, thinking. Did the dream mean something or was it nonsense?

I went down to the kitchen, feeling the need to get out of bed. I opened and closed the refrigerator door multiple times. I was not hungry, I just didn't know what to do with myself. I went and sat at the kitchen table, tapping my fingernails against the surface of it. I then quietly opened the sliding glass door that led to the back yard. I closed it, bored. Finally, I turned on the television and immediately lowered the volume so it would not wake anybody. I watched an infomercial for an exercise machine that was sure to make every muscle in your body strong, or something like that.

I watched the man with bulging arms, shoulders, and torso lift up and down one of the bars on the machine with mild interest. He was too muscular to be attractive to me. I let the dream sit comfortably in my head. I was too tired to actively think about it. As I watched the man use the fancy machine I hoped my brain was hard at work figuring out the dream, if there was anything to figure out. Then my eyes popped opened wide, I was awake. Could it be that the castle and cove were the same thing? Could it be that what determined if I was able to get into the cove or not depended on how I approached it?

The question caused both my mind and body to awaken. My mind buzzed. There had to be a parallel. The first time I went to the cove it opened with no problems. I had expected nothing and was delighted when it opened. The second time, when I had been eager and hurried, the cove opened eventually, but not right away. The third time I had been demanding, anxious, and expectant, and the cove did not open at all.

Was there an intuition in this dream that I hadn't come across in my waking life? I wondered how many revelations I missed simply by not remembering dreams. I would work on changing my mindset for approaching the cove. I fell asleep on the couch, watching oiled, bulging arms.

The next day I went out and looked at the chalk rainbow. No mist or rain had disturbed it. I flashed back to the past again. My spirits lifted and I knew I was looking at some kind of truth. It was a covenant, but what kind of covenant could this be?

But then I knew. Was it was from a religion? No, it was more than religion. It wasn't from something purely Christian, or Jewish, or Islamic, or Buddhist, or any religion that existed on Earth. Those things were too small for this covenant. The rainbow, I knew in my heart, with overwhelming peace, was a covenant between God, in whatever form God existed, and people. I had learned this once, and it was embedded in my soul.

This gave an alternate to my depression. The peace I felt was as strong as my despair. It was as pure and absolute as the despair. The peace and despair did not mix. When I felt the despair, late at night when I held that necklace in my hand, it was all I felt. I could feel it coming and the sadness encroaching in on me and I would take the heart, hold it tight in my hand and the sadness would infiltrate my soul. But then I would wake up the next morning, forgetting about the necklace in the abandon of sleep. I always woke up knowing there was a promise for me, one that you could find in a rainbow. Even though I did not know what the promise was, that did not matter. As I thought only of the promise the sadness was at bay, waiting outside of me, at my feet. It was waiting to attack but in those moments, it was unable to. It would come back, but thinking of that chalk rainbow, and the nebulous covenant that it belonged to helped me keep moving forward.

Twenty-one

I did not tell anyone about my dream, but I thought about it a lot. Cale agreed to go with me to the cove the next week. As I thought of the cove, and of God, I was humbled. I was one little person in the world, and the cove was beyond what I could have imagined. When the day approached we drove to the same spot and got out and followed the creek. As we walked I knew I did not own the cove and it was not mine. I thought of the wonder of it. Surely there was someone, somewhere, who had taken the time to construct these binders, to follow me, to be a part of me.

When we got to the stump the next week, there were two mugs of tomato soup on it and two small loaves of bread. I laughed in an outburst of joy. Cale looked unsurprised and I supposed the shock of the last time was enough to cover this time too.

"Cale, let's eat!"

I tore off a piece of bread and dipped it into the hot tomato soup. As soon as it was in my mouth I had a strong memory. I was in a church. There was an alter with a silver chalice on it and a silver plate with a loaf of bread that was torn into two. There was a line of people in front of the two people who were holding the chalice and plate. Then I stood in front of those two people. I watched my hands tear of a piece of bread and dip it into the chalice. I put my hand under bread to keep the crimson purple bread from dripping on the floor. The bread, soaked in juice, was sweet and delicious. That moment was one of pure peace and it was in my entire being. This time I saw that the wonder was inside of a religion, but I knew no religion could ever contain the enchanted nature of the God that must exist.

For just a moment I felt this enchanted Creator wholly. In that moment everything made sense. In that moment love felt boundless. I was grateful for everything. I felt very small. The plan for my life was much bigger than what I could see. I knew my struggles would ultimately help me. Life came with great responsibility. I had to use my life well.

This intricate feeling was only a flash but I was left with deep peace. I was left knowing there was a reason I was in the world. I was left with knowing every person had as much right and reason to be in the world with me. It was God. The cove was somehow God.

Water ran down the rock. We cleaned out our mugs, filled them with water, and drank. We filled our mugs again and then the water dried up. I went to the stump and saw the hinges, door handle, and rectangular outline on the stump. I filled with contentment. I lifted the door, gently laying it on the edge of the stump. I went down and looked at the precariously stacked binders. I did not know where to start, nor did I know my depression was going to get worse before it got better.

I wondered about the necklace and the boy who had given it to me. I must have been nine or ten when I got it, if my fleeting memory was correct. I told Cale about the memory and we decided to start looking in the nine and ten-year-old stacks. I took the nines and Cale took the tens. We took the first ones outside the cove to look at them.

In the nine years and three months binder I saw a newspaper clipping that triggered a memory. The newspaper clipping was about a fire that had destroyed a house. It did not identify the family but I knew it had been my family's house. The article said the family was unharmed but their dog had been trapped inside and died. Then I remembered my beloved dog, Cowboy. I remembered the feelings of desperation and helplessness. I remembered standing in the front yard and my mother grasping me. I wanted to go inside and get my dog. I was distressed about what was going to inevitably happen to him.

I faintly remembered the smell of smoke and the haziness in the air. I remembered not seeing flames, only smoke rising into the air like steam from a pot. I remembered a fire truck and ambulance. I remembered people yelling. I did not remember the specifics of what had been said, but I remembered my own panic. I mostly remembered the visceral, the things that invaded my senses. The smell would have been quite nice in a fireplace. The smoke detector had beeped, the first sign of danger. It was like an alarm clock I could not turn off. In my sleep I was angry at the beeping, not wanting to wake up, only half hearing it. The sleep, in the beginning, was more powerful than the attack to my senses.

I remembered the feeling of losing my identity after the fire. It was a vague feeling and hard to grasp, but I was certain it was there. I no longer had the possessions I once called mine, the ones I had owned and treated with care and that surrounded me in my bedroom. I could no longer recreate the familiarity of sitting on the steps of my front porch, watching cars go by while alternately looking at the familiar slats of wood that made up the steps.

Although I could not remember many specifics I did remember the loss of Cowboy. The loss had shattered something in me. I imagined his pain, his suffering, the fear he must have felt in those last moments. Had it hurt? Had he been scared? I hoped that it was the smoke that killed him, not the fire. I hoped it was peaceful, as though he were just going to sleep. I wanted to know where he was now. Had he simply ceased to exist? Was his spirit gone and destroyed like the items in the house that were gone and destroyed? I missed him but even more than that I was scared for him. Was someone taking care of him? I had prayed he was not alone in the great void of death.

I knew the fire changed my life, that I no longer felt safe when I went to bed at night. I knew that as I fell to sleep I remembered the loud, insistent beep of the smoke detector that had woken me up that night. I remembered the rough shaking awake by my father as he told me with urgency, "The house is on fire." That I remembered being outside, surrounded by dark air and smoke.

As I thought of this image of standing outside, memories came in an avalanche. At first, until everything changed again, I clung to my parents, constantly afraid of losing them. In quick succession after the fire I did lose them. It was not physically, and it was not complete, but it was more heartbreaking than the fire.

The clarity and specifics of the memories coming back were more extensive than any I had before. I remembered after the fire we moved into the house of family friends. I did not remember the parents and only vaguely remembered the daughter, who was an older teenager. It was Corey, the one who gave me the necklace, who I remembered. Corey was tall and wore jeans and striped shirts. He was cool and paid attention to me at a time when I felt forgotten. My parents worked and were preoccupied with the mess of the fire and the business of finding a new place to live. His sister was immersed in her high school life, sports, homework, boys, and general teenage happenings. She barely talked to me. I missed my dog and after the fire I felt so separate from my friends.

Corey paid attention to me, and it was a relief someone did. Knowing there was someone paying attention made me less scared. Corey played board games and card games with me, Monopoly, Uno, War. He let me tell him about the kids at school I liked and didn't like. He would walk with me to the convenient store near his house, where he would get a Coke

Icee. I always filled mine up with half Coke and half Cherry, putting the clear dome shaped plastic top on the Icee cup first and then filling it so high it overflowed. He always paid for both of them with his allowance. Corey made me feel good and I felt less lonely when I was around him.

One day Corey told me I was sweet. Two days later he said I was beautiful. That was when he gave me the necklace, acting as though it were no big deal, telling me he had stolen it just because he could. He said for a kid I was okay and so I could have it. I treasured the gold colored necklace with the small heart hanging off it. We were usually home alone after school while our parents were still at work and his sister was at basketball practice. One day I got off the bus, feeling important that all the traffic had to stop just for me, and went into the house, throwing my backpack down beside the staircase like I always did.

My first order of business was always to get a snack, Corey too. When I went into the kitchen, Corey was there, sitting at the table with the pizza box from the night before sitting in front of him. I sat opposite to him and helped myself to a slice of pepperoni.

When we both finished eating there was a lull and he was staring at me. Something was wrong. I did not know what to do, his eyes were so intense. I could not bring myself to break eye contact. I became rigid and nervous. I made my body perfectly symmetrical. My feet were right beside each other on the floor. The backs of my knees touched the chair in identical places. My back was straight and I leaned forward slightly. My elbows were bent and they rested on the table. My hands were balled into fists and propped under my chin.

"I want to show you something in the bathroom," he told me. I was in a trance, still looking into his eyes. I walked across the stark, unfriendly, tiled floor and into the large bathroom. Corey followed closely and when we were both in the bathroom he closed the door behind him. I felt a little uncomfortable but thought I was being silly. Corey was my friend, he was my favorite.

He said, "This is a picture I painted," alluding to a framed painting on the wall. "It's from kindergarten. I know it's not good, but it's been hanging here ever since then. The painting was large. To get it home I imagined a teacher must have carefully rolled it up, keeping it in good condition. It must have not stayed in young Corey's hands for long, the paper was uncreased.

It was a colorful painting of a house, "It's this house," he said. I felt sad about my house then. Corey was proud of his painting, I could tell. He pretended to think it was stupid that it was hanging in the bathroom, but there was a lilt in his voice when he told me it had been hanging there since kindergarten. A lilt that said, 'somebody thought I was worth something then.'

"I think my mom hung it up," he said. I smiled, just barely, to myself. It was not really anything special, but he seemed vulnerable in that moment. Even to my nine-year-old self, it was endearing. I relaxed, appreciating that it was eye-catching and its colors, rich.

I turned to the door as I said, "It's nice." He turned away from the painting and toward me. In a swoop he picked me up by the waist. I was suspended in the air, strong hands gripping my waist tight, and my eyes were a few inches from the painting.

"The sun," he said, "Is my favorite part." I was so close to the painting that it was hard to see that the mass of lines made a picture. I could see the sun's imperfect circle just above my eye line though, and the rays, an afterthought, were reckless. My eyes filled with tears, I wanted to be let down, let go, and to be far away from that bathroom. I wanted to be alone.

"I want to get down," I said, my mouth moving but no voice coming out. Corey's hands tightened around my waist as he let me down. My feet were on the floor. He let me go and stood up straight. He loomed between the door and me. I still faced the wall, unsure of what was happening. Tears were falling quickly and silently from my eyes. I did not know why I was crying. I wanted to go somewhere nobody could see me.

I heard the bathroom door lock. His fingers ran from the base of my back and up, going underneath my shirt. I could only remember the parts where he seemed especially bold, the parts where I started to disappear. I started to disappear as he turned me around by my shoulders, when I was face to face with his crotch, when he unzipped his pants, let them fall to the ground. I disappeared more when he took my hand, guided my hand into the hole in his plaid boxers. He was soft until my hand touched him. Then he was hard, and I was scared, much more scared than I had been during the fire. I disappeared more when he dropped his boxers and told me to kiss him there, where my hand had been. Then he gently took my shoes off and told me he wanted to see what I looked like under my clothes. I took this as an order and took my pants off. I took my pants off instead of my shirt because my legs were farther away from the speaking voice, and at least I had on panties. The bathroom was so big, and undressing did not foreshadow for me that we would be laying down on it, I was too young to know that. Corey bent down on his knees and reached toward my hips.

"No!" I said, surprisingly loudly. I felt very meek. He ignored me. He slid my panties down and I obediently lifted each foot up for him. It was as though I had said nothing. In my 9-year-old body I felt him touch where my panties had been and then his hands reach under my shirt to my undeveloped breasts. I thought that was bad but then it got much worse. I barely knew what sex was, and even after he had sex with me, I didn't really know what had happened. My clothes were on the floor and it hurt, so bad, down there. There was blood everywhere and I was still bleeding.

"You're so sweet," he said. I disappeared completely. There was no trace of me there. Yet the whole time, I was thoroughly there. Afterward I lay curled up on the bathroom floor. I wore only my shirt and socks. I was as far away from the blood as I could get.

"You should put your clothes back on," he said with a hint of concern and urgency. He watched me as I picked up my jeans and panties, both of which had blood on them. I put them on anyway. I carried my shoes, which had remained blood-free, in my hand. I stepped out of the bathroom, tiptoeing over the pool of blood. I took off my socks, which I hadn't kept completely away from the blood. I went upstairs and immediately took off my clothes and panties. Putting on more clothes as soon as I could, not wanting to be naked. I balled my clothes up, making sure the blood was all on the inside of the ball, and put them under my mattress, with the plan to throw them away later.

I got under my covers, hurting. I was so small and he was so big. Later, when I pulled down my pants and panties I would see that there was more blood there. I resolved to throw those clothes away too. Nothing had gotten on the sheets but I layered towels on top of the bed to keep any blood off them.

It had all lasted minutes, but I did not really move for years.

When my mom got home, later, she found me in bed and asked me what was wrong. If she did not know, Corey must have cleaned up the blood.

"I'm sick," I said. She felt my forehead, looking concerned.

"You feel okay," my mom said, "But I'll take your temperature." I didn't have a temperature, but I shivered, and did not eat my dinner. I always ate. The next day I went to school as if nothing had happened. Something had died in me in that bathroom, and the lack of hesitation of the world cemented it.

I cried in the bathroom stall the next day, but nobody saw me. That night I held the heart on the necklace tight in my hand. I had taken the necklace off when I had taken my bloody clothes off. I kept it under my pillow. I was unable to get rid of it even though I hated it. It became my nearest companion. I needed to know there was something that knew my secret. I became an expert at seeming okay. I learned too well how easy it is for a child to seem okay.

As the memories flowed through my mind I understood the question from my dreams, 'Do you ever see anything other than bodies?' It was because for years after this incident I connected with nobody. I lived life as an obligation and my world was internal. Looking back I could not comprehend why I never told anyone. The emotional pain was deep enough that it was physical. I remembered enough to know that all those years ago I watched it happen to myself, the way I disappeared. I saw it all, yet I seemed to have no control.

I did know, in a way, why I never told anyone. In my mind Corey cared about me, and that was why he did it. I had needed to feel loved and I could not risk the cessation of love from him or anyone I might have told. The pain of what happened was pain I would take into myself. The loss of love would have been a far worse pain.

Despite this, I kept the necklace. I didn't wear it, but I kept it in safe places. I did not know why I hung on to it, but maybe it was because it held my secret and a massive experience. If the necklace was with me, perhaps I could contain it. Even then, after finding it in the binder, it was the only real thing I had from the past. It was the only physical object I could hold in my hand. I knew at some point I must have gotten rid of it. Surely that was the only way it could have ended up in the binder, right?

As I stood outside the cove all those years later, I did not feel peace anymore. I was no longer sure if anything good existed. I was shocked at how quickly and completely my memories of this had come back and I could feel other memories were there. They needed work to be drawn out though. It felt that my brain was collapsing from the weight of all I had remembered and I did not have the energy to do anything else, not at that moment. The promises of memories faded as I sunk deeper in depression.

"Cale, I remember, I know what happened all those years ago." I did not tell him though.

"Are you okay?" he asked. I must not have looked okay. It seemed that everything had changed, not just my memories, but who I was. I was that little girl again, the one who had been lost in a void of pain.

"Yes," I said, hiding it in the same way I had all those years ago. I didn't know why I was so intent on keeping this to myself, but I knew I did not want to feel more vulnerable than I already did.

My 'yes,' carried with it many other words. Words I did not know how to string together. They were in front of me, bumping together and pushing apart. How would I ever make them understandable, these words I did not know how to get from my mind to my mouth. There was a kind of torment in my mind that I wanted to resolve right away, while there was someone in front of me to listen. It felt urgent, because I knew later I would be alone with my thoughts. There was nothing to say though, it simply was. Nobody would feel it but me, no matter how much I wanted another to understand it.

If this had happened then surely it was in the binders. I considered finding this experience in the binders and showing Cale the facts. That seemed to be the next best option to trying to find the words to describe it. And I did find it in the next binder. I liked the black and white of it. The simplicity, the way the situation was reported anchored me. I knew if I showed Cale the unmistakable facts in that black and white it may seem like I was unaffected, like I had come across something difficult, but not necessarily painful. Maybe it would make it seem that the emotion attached to it was dull, that I had gotten out of it unscathed. I did not show him, however, I did not want it to be easy. I did not want to put it out there as though it were nothing. I closed the binder and took them all back down.

Twenty-two

The memory of Corey served as a trigger to a full-scale destruction of my emotional self. Metaphorically, it was as though there was a big pipe, a cylinder that ran from my neck through my stomach. The pipe had been filling with depression certainly, but I managed to fit goodness in there too. The pipe held my soul. Because there was good in the pipe, I was able to see good in myself, in others, and in the world. After remembering that day and all that came after, the pipe became hollow. The happiness I had was sucked out of me. Without this pipe – my core, holding goodness, my body felt empty of anything other than the flesh, tissue, and blood that make up a human. Deep fears manifested themselves. I began to believe without doubt I was unworthy and unloved, and had always been.

Love became everything I could possibly need and I had no way to get it. The receptors on my body that absorbed love particles shrunk to almost nothing. They were malfunctioning in the same way receptors in my brain must have been malfunctioning. I was able to take in the smallest hope from what could only be God. I wanted someone to understand this change in me more than I wanted to breathe.

I became that nine-year-old girl and my needs intensified. I wanted someone to simply put their hand on my arm. My life seemed doomed and my thinking veered into the catastrophic. Things would never be better, I was sure. The pain was incredibly deep and my thinking reached a point of having barely an ounce of logic in it. It was foggily visible but I knew God, the God that must exist, was there somewhere and eventually, the pain would leave. I believed at some point in my life I must have done something good and that had to be enough for me. Even if nobody knew me, I had to believe in some way, I mattered.

It was shocking, how I shot to severe depression in no time at all. I remembered the rainbow, and I remembered goodness, but that didn't seem to help. That whole time I had awareness of what was happening to me. I was fighting, and fighting hard. I fought every feeling and even though God must have wanted me to live, fighting and losing was exhausting to the point I stopped caring. My pain and exhaustion were engulfing and all I experienced. Nothing else in the world mattered. I lost the ability to see beyond myself and I entered a world that was all my own.

The day after I went to the cove and had these memories, Jennifer's Restaurant called me. They were looking for some morning help, and were wondering if I could come in the next day with my ID and Social Security Card. This only contributed to my despair. I didn't have an ID or Social Security Card. "Sure," I said though, determined to talk them into letting me work there.

Late that night though, I lay in bed, unable to sleep and not knowing how to bear the pain. This had gone beyond the memories, beyond Corey and I felt unequivocally that there was something off in my brain. about my brain. It was as though something had been activated in me. True, something legitimately had been taken from me all those years ago, but that is not what unhinged me. That had served to prompt to life a very deep problem that must have been living inside me, all that time.

By the time it started to get light outside and I had not slept all night, I knew a kind of sadness I could not have imagined. By sunrise I was only a fraction of myself. I had become small and weak. Staying awake all night was one of the most destructive things I could have done. Sleep was restorative and put everything from the day before a shade away. And I didn't have that.

I heard moving downstairs and decided to go down, hoping it would get me out of my head. I sat up in bed and put my feet on the floor, as I did I remembered sitting on the edge of the hospital bed. I began to hyperventilate. The amount of air I needed seemed limitless and no matter how much I gulped it did not seem like enough. I remembered the job at Jennifer's and knew it was pointless. They wouldn't hire me. I sat down on the floor and saw a spider in the corner. Everything was sordid. I could see the stairs from where I sat. They looked hazy through my sleep-deprived eyes, and I knew what I had to do. I became calm. I walked to the top of the stairs and stood on my tiptoes. I fell.

I heard screaming. It was Kristen, "Oh my God. Oh my God! Can you hear me? Ella!? Are you ok?"

'Let me begin again,' I thought, 'I want the brokenness to go away. How I wish I could start over and for everything to be right.'

I could walk, but it was painful. Cale drove me to the hospital. I had three broken toes, a broken arm, a mild concussion, and many bruises. They put a cast on my arm and splints on my toes. I told no one that I had fallen on purpose, that I was attempting to silence the screaming pain and confusion. I told no one I was trying to stop thinking. I was scared. I did not want to die. I just wanted everything in my head to stop. I forgot to, or maybe couldn't, take all the chaos and put it aside, like I had done before. With the pain medicine at the hospital, finally, I fell asleep. When I woke up, I was alone, still in the hospital, and I was angry. I was angry at

Corey and at myself. He had no right to do what he had done and I had no right to let myself still be victimized.

I grasped my hand around the heart on the chain around my neck and pulled it hard, pulling off the necklace and threw it across the room. The most wondrous thing happened. All the pain drained out of my body and I felt all the things that I thought had deserted me. I understood the reason the necklace was in my twenty-one-year binder, the year Corey died. That was when I fully let it go, that was when I stopped letting him have power over me. That was when I was proactive, shielding myself from pain, instead of reactive, responding to pain. When I discovered it in the binder, I did not remember what the necklace meant. I went near the necklace and looked closer at it, it was on the floor, but I didn't touch it. Was it a locket? Yes, it was. It was not just any heart, it looked like a locket, but I would have to pick it up to be sure.

I picked it up and looked closely at the heart that was rounded on both sides. I felt a heaviness descend upon me, and I understood that this necklace was dangerous. It was laced with pain that had threatened my life. It had a tiny prong on the outside and I pressed it and it opened. But there was no picture, nothing inside it at all. In so many ways, it was full of emptiness.

Something was happening but I did not know what. Then everything bad seeped into my skin. Everything I had felt as I stood at the top of the stairs was back in me, completely pure. Was this real? Was there really something about the necklace that held sadness in it? I closed the locket and dropped it on the floor. The sadness disappeared. I went back to the bed and looked at the necklace across the room. It was in a place that nobody would notice but I would be able to retrieve when I was ready.

I wanted to do something grand, smash it with a hammer and throw it into a landfill. Maybe drop it into a sewer where it would be picked up and run over by rats. Maybe bury it deep in the ground. Maybe throw it into the ocean. While I knew I would get a certain kind of symbolic relief from these things I decided instead to keep it. I would put in the back of my closet, I would be able to see it, keep an eye on it, but it would have no way to reach me, to touch my skin, to infect me. In the meantime I would keep it with me. I would keep in the hospital room with me with me until I got home. Shortly after I woke up the doctor came in.

"You had a bad fall," the doctor said, "but you're going to be just fine. You're fine to go, the nurse will discharge you in a few minutes." The doctor told me to take it easy, and to be more careful. When the doctor walked out of the room I went to the corner and picked up the necklace. Then a nurse came in and gave me discharge papers and made an appointment for a follow up visit to get the cast on my arm off. I laid the necklace on the paper and then folded the paper around it as many times as I could. I could feel sadness ramping up, and wondered how to best protect myself. I laid it on the bedside table and used the phone to call the house. Kristen answered and I told her I could leave – she and Cale had stepped out after the first couple of hours into my hospital stay. She said she would pick me up. I told her I'd wait outside.

I was wheeled out to the front in a wheelchair, which seemed unnecessary. The closer I got to the exit the more amazed I became that someone was not barring my way. They did not know though, that I had meant to fall down the stairs. The necklace was in my pocket and I couldn't wait to get it out. I knew I would become increasingly pessimistic and unhappy until I got it out. I made it home though, without dipping too far into despair, the necklace wasn't touching my skin.

When I got home I went straight to my bedroom and to the closet, slowing making my way slowly on the heel of my foot, keeping my toes protected. As I unfolded the paper and then put the necklace on the floor I was sad for the girl who had borne that tragedy alone. I was sad for the girl who was woven into a tornado of sadness. When I pulled that necklace off I had been thrown out and the pain of the landing was incidental. It would have been much more dangerous to have been drawn into that cyclone deeper and deeper.

After the necklace was in the back of my closet I realized how easily I had started breathing. It seemed so natural. It was hard to remember what it felt like to not get enough air. I thought of the puddle, the water I had choked on in the forest. I marveled at how only when you were on the inside of a situation could you feel its intensity. Was it possible for someone on the outside to feel something with the same intensity as someone living in the skin of an experience? What a marvelous thought, for someone to be connected with you that intimately, but that pain, what would it do to them?

Twenty-three

I called Kalyn and told her about my fall. I asked if she wanted to come over, that I would love to see a friendly face. So she came to visit me. She brought me a puzzle. I laughed at this, believing I was much too old or much too young for a puzzle. It was not just any puzzle either, it was a five-thousand-piece puzzle. It was a puzzle of the United States and it was unexpectedly enjoyable. We sat on my bed while Kalyn was there. I leaned on a pillow propped against the headboard and she sat on the other end of the bed. I put the open puzzle box between us and we picked out edge pieces as we talked. The distraction made me braver, and with the lack of eye contact between us, I told deeper truths than I had intended.

"I meant to fall down the stairs," I said in a peculiar celebration of finding a corner piece. Then there was silence. My words seemed to permeate the air and coat the walls. What a heavy thing to say. It sat between us, like the puzzle did. Kalyn looked at me with what appeared to be curiosity but did not say anything. The longer those words sat there the less of its weight I held. Kalyn kept picking edge pieces out of the box and so did I.

"I'm glad you're okay," she said, examining one of the pieces. I heard warmth in her voice.

"I am," I said, "I really am."

Kalyn smiled at me. "If at any point you're not okay, let me or someone else know, would you?"

"Yes," I said softly, "I will try my best to escape any future tornados."

I told her about the job at Jennifer's, and how I simply hadn't shown up because of the accident, and how I needed an ID and Social Security Card. "It's pointless," I told her, feeling defeated. She encouraged me to call them, to explain I had been in the hospital, and ask if they still needed someone. Maybe, I began to think, this could work, and I could do this still.

I told Kalyn I hadn't been working on the stories, not even Sydney's much. That I had been spending my days trying to sleep because I wasn't sleeping at night. That I had been taking aimless walks around the neighborhood. That my time had been disappearing, I hadn't been doing anything, but time was passing somehow. I told her that was going to change though. That very day, it was going to change. Tragedy no longer dictated my life.

After Kalyn left I called Jennifer's Restaurant and fumbled my way through an explanation that I had been in the hospital, but was perfectly fine – I vehemently assured them – and that's why I hadn't shown up two days before. If they still needed someone, I told them, I would be very interested in working there in the mornings. Before breaking the news, I had no ID or Social Security Card, I needed them to tell me they still wanted me there. They did still need help! They asked if I could I come that afternoon, to fill out some paperwork. "Yes, of course!" I said with what probably seemed like a supreme amount of enthusiasm. I felt infinitely lighter than I had just two days before.

I looked at the clock as I said this. It was almost 2:30pm. With my broken toes, there was no way I would get there before five. I thought of my determination to always walk on my own and not let anyone help me, my solid belief I had before that I was an adult and needed to act and be treated like one.

I got off the couch and went upstairs to my bedroom. I looked in the full-length mirror on my door. I took in my cast. My shoeless, bandaged foot. My eyes bored into my forehead. Just past that layer of skin and bone stood my brain. The brain that had just been given a mild concussion. The brain that had once been full of so much pain that it was now empty of, the full territory of it, now, hope. The brain that had tormented me during this depression. I looked at my face and into my eyes. I stepped closer, still looking into my eyes. I wondered how far down they went into who I was. I broke my gaze and walked away, I had seen in my eyes that it was okay to ask for help. I made my way down the stairs and into Cale's office.

"Cale, Jennifer's Restaurant needs someone for the mornings and they will hire me if I can convince them that I don't need an ID or Social Security Card. They want me to come by this afternoon, do you think you could give me a ride?"

Cale smiled at me, "That's great Ella," he was genuine. "Of course I'll take you."

Quickly though, he looked puzzled. "You can work there with a broken arm and three broken toes?" I was washed over with shame. What had I done to myself? I looked at the floor, studying the rug. 'No,' I thought firmly, 'it's what I will do for myself now.'

My body and soul became even lighter, I was beginning again.

Twenty-four

On the drive to the restaurant I apologized to Cale for letting the story slide. "I want to work on it though. I've met Sydney's friends, I've met her family, I've looked at cards she was given, this is important to me." In a humble moment I asked, "Can we talk this over so I can get started again?"

"Yes, Ella, just focus on the restaurant right now, we can talk about this when we get back home."

I hobbled out of the car and into the restaurant, we had quickly gotten there. I was thankful that my left arm had been broken, and not my right, since I was right-handed, that would certainly help my success in writing down orders. Besides, the place hadn't looked too busy the morning I had been there before.

I went to the deserted cash register and looked around for someone who worked there. A woman wearing a 'Jennifer's Restaurant' t-shirt was standing at the only occupied table with her back to me. Between three broken toes, one broken arm, no

ID, and no Social Security Card, this was going to be an uphill climb. As she turned around I caught her attention.

"Hi, my name is Ella. I had applied for a job and Marie asked me to come to fill out some paperwork."

"Yes, I'm Marie. Well, we do need to hire someone right away, one of our morning girls is leaving and we don't have a replacement. She's leaving in a week, but we need someone to train before she leaves. I'm ready to hire someone today... but... what did you do to yourself?"

"Oh, this?" I asked, nodding to my arm. She looked at my arm, and then looked at my foot. "Oh yeah," I said, feigning obliviousness, "That too. Well, these are just minor problems, really, I don't think they will affect my work at all." Marie, who looked to be about 50, raised her eyebrows. Her light brown bob fell in front of her face as she looked down at my foot again.

"Do you have any experience?" she asked, looking back up at me.

"Um… well, nobutimafastlearner." It was a statement that all came out at once. I wanted to throw in that I was a fast learner as soon as possible after saying 'no.' Marie paused.

"We really need someone. Do you think you could start tomorrow? We can try it out, I suppose."

"YES I CAN START TOMORROW." My voice sounded very loud and several people looked at me.

"Ok, calm down now," Marie said. "Did you bring your ID and Social Security Card?"

I had won half the battle, I had to stay focused though, this was even more important.

"That could be a problem. I don't have an ID or Social Security Card."

"Of course you do," she stated without hesitation. "You mean you lost them?" I saw gold in this statement. This was my opportunity.

"Yes," I lied. Technically, in a way, that was true.

"Well we can't hire you without those. I'm sorry."

"I'm completely legal to work and old enough. I promise!"

"Have you ever been arrested?" she asked.

"No."

"How old are you?"

"20."

"I must say that's pretty irresponsible to lose both your ID and Social Security Card. You know, you can get replacements."

"Yes," I said, rolling with it. "That's what I was planning to do."

"Hold on," she said. "Let me go get the owner." I didn't know if this was a good or bad development.

"Jennifer came out in stained Jennifer's t-shirt."

"Awww, she looks fine," she said, "You're planning on getting replacement cards?"

"Yes," I said with a million cords of happy music playing behind my voice.

"Just hire her. We'll pay her under the table for now." I could barely believe what was happening. I paid no mind to how I would possibly be able to prove my identity to get an ID and Social Security Card.

"Okay," said Marie. "Come in tomorrow at 6:00 am." Then, just like that it was over.

"Okay," I said. "Thanks. I'll see you tomorrow."

I'm not here in the mornings. You will be training with Vanessa. She's the one who's about to leave. You get paid $2.13 an hour. The rest comes from tips." This stopped me short. I didn't know what the minimum wage was, but that seemed pretty low. I wasn't going to complain though. I had a job!

I walked out to the car calmly, but at this point, the music playing in my body was deafening. How could things go from so bad to so good?

Cale saw me approaching and rolled down the window as I walked toward the car.

"How did it go?" he called out.

"Cale. Oh my gosh. I got the job. They actually hired me despite having a broken arm, broken toes, and no identification of any kind. I opened the door and hopped into the front seat."

Cale smirked as he pulled the car out of the lot.

"Cale, what?"

"You're just so excited. It's funny."

"It's just… I really needed this. I really need to feel like I can do something on my own. I don't want to rely on everyone for everything. This makes me feel like a real adult."

"Well good," Cale said. "When do you start?"

"Tomorrow."

"Wow. You said this was the morning shift?"

"Yeah. I have to be there tomorrow at 6:00."

"Oh, that's early."

"Well, they open at 6:30."

"Ok, Kristen or I will take you."

"No," I said halfheartedly, "I'll walk."

"Ella, you are not walking all the way over here with three broken toes when it's not even light yet. One of us will take you." Kristen was not going to like this, I knew. I was relieved that he offered though. I didn't want to have to attempt to walk in cold, pitch-black air in the early morning hours."

"Ok, thanks Cale. That will be really helpful. I'll find my own way back."

"That's fine, Ella."

Twenty-five

Working for Jennifer's Diner turned out to be very good for me. My hours were the morning shift Tuesday through Saturday. When I got there in the mornings I started right away, rolling silverware, putting the nozzles back on the soda machine, putting ketchup on the tables, and starting the coffee. There were only two of us there that early. I quickly realized there were regulars, people who came in every morning. They mostly all got coffee and I started pouring it into mugs for them as soon as I saw them coming in the door. They had patterns with their orders, but I knew it would take me a while to remember what they all ordered.

Through that job, for that few weeks, I realized that I could be pretty outgoing and was even good at small talk and joking. My shifts were busy, but not too busy, the flow was just right. I ended my shifts at 12:00, tired but happy and on the walk home I relaxed, letting the work leave me and moving into the next part of the day. The job felt like the beginning of a new chapter for me, moving forward toward independence instead of dependency. The first week was an adjustment, but one I was thrilled about. I liked my schedule, it was predictable and solid.

When I got home after that first day and walked across the freshly cut grass in the front yard, I added Sydney to the mix of thoughts in my mind.

When I got in the house I called Kalyn.

"Guess what?! I got the job!" I told her.

"So you convinced them to hire you, huh?"

I laughed, "Yes, it's a miracle."

"I'm excited for you, congratulations!"

After several more minutes on the phone we hung up and I went into Cale's office.

"Alright Cale, let's talk this whole Sydney thing over."

"Okay Ella, tell me where you are with things now."

I went through everything I had done – calling and meeting Martha, meeting Sydney's friends, finding out that Courtney was Ella's daughter, and getting the cards from Martha.

"What are you planning on doing next?" he asked.

"I should probably write up what I can before going any further and then reassess."

It seemed like I had come up with that solution easily, Cale had asked a good, if simple, question to get me to that decision.

And so I started to write. I found myself befuddled with the level of perfection that I felt it needed to be done at. But then I remembered when I had anxiety about that very thing before and the conclusion I had come to then. It didn't have to be perfect, it just had to be done. I had to start somewhere, it could become better over time.

What I did was similar to free writing, or even a journal entry. I wrote down all I had learned so far. It brought me to thoughts of Courtney, and how she too had been through something very difficult, the death of her mother, even though she thought Sydney was her sister. I decided to ask Martha if she needed a babysitter sometime, no cost. I called Martha and offered my services, and told her I would love to connect with

Courtney. Martha said I could meet them at the park by their house the next afternoon, that Courtney would much rather go to the park than run errands with her. It was too far to walk so Kristen took me. I was at the park before they got there and the longer I waited the more nervous I became. When Martha came I had polite words with her, and she said she would be back in a couple of hours.

Courtney was very quiet at first, but within a couple of minutes she saw her friend Stuart and went to play with him. After half an hour Stuart left. Courtney stayed on the swing where they had been, and I went to join her. I sat on the swing next to her and dug my heel into the sand. I looked over at Courtney. She was still, just sitting on the swing staring at the ground in front of her. I kicked off with both my heels and started swinging. I got as high as I could go and for a moment I forgot about Courtney. It felt familiar, nostalgic even. I could not remember ever swinging before, but surely I had.

I let the swing slow and looked at Courtney, weighing my words. "Come on, swing! It's fun," I said, smiling at her.

"Please." She looked over and gave me the faintest smile. She started swinging, just a little, but I felt like something had been accomplished. Suddenly Courtney bolted out of the swing and started running. She ran across the park and behind the house next door. I walked as fast as I could, able to walk more quickly than I ran, limited by my broken toes. I went to the back of the house where I had seen her go, but did not see her anywhere.

I yelled her name but only heard a dog barking in the distance. I called her name again and after waiting a few seconds I heard her voice.

"Over here," she said. She popped around the corner of the house. "Come in here." I ducked between the two bushes. The ground was worn. "This is my fort." I wondered if the owners of the house knew about this fort. "I like you," she said, which surprised me, since she did not seem to notice me much before. I was unsure if I should bring up Sydney, but felt a sort of camaraderie with Courtney at the moment.

"I'm sorry about your sister, Courtney."

"She was my mama," Courtney responded. Immediately she threw her hands over her mouth and her eyes became wide.

She stayed like that until I said, "It's ok, I won't tell anyone you know."

She took her hands off her mouth. "I meant to tell you but then I thought maybe it was the wrong thing to do."

I looked into her child eyes and asked, "How do you know Sydney is your mama?"

"I saw a picture. Sydney was in the hospital and she was holding a baby. I asked her who it was and she said it was me. That's when she told me she was my mama, but I wasn't supposed to know so I couldn't tell anyone. I wish she hadn't told me."

"Why not?" I asked, impressed that she seemed to have kept the secret from Martha.

"Because I can't tell anyone and it's inside me and it makes me feel like nobody knows me. You're the only person who knows."

I thought of how destructive keeping a secret had been for me as a girl the same age as Courtney. Although this secret was not quite as sinister as mine had been it was still uncomfortably inside her and made her feel like nobody knew her all the way. I was not sure if it was very often that a secret was a good thing.

"I'm glad you told me," I said. "At least one person can know that you know. You are brave and strong to keep a secret like that." We lapsed into silence. "Let's go back to the playground," I said. As we walked back Courtney grabbed my hand and held it loosely, but surely. Once back to the playground she scampered off to the slide. She climbed the steps, lingering at the top, sitting at the edge of the descent, unmoving. I took a step back from the slide, and she gripped its edges, preparing to send herself down. She slid down gracefully and hopped off. As she ran back to the top I turned and walked to the merry-go-round and sat on its curved edge. At the top she looked at me as she again sat at the top of the slide. After she went down and hopped off, she stood, facing my direction. She seemed to spot something on the ground between her and me. She walked toward me and when she was halfway to me she bent to the ground and picked a blade of grass.

"Can I show you something?" she asked.

"Sure," I said.

"Watch this," she said as she came toward me, "I can make this into a whistle." She situated the grass between her thumbs, pulling it tight. She blew on the grass, which was turned on its edge, but it did not make a noise. She looked at it, a wisp of embarrassment lay bare on her face.

"Let me try," I said gently, she would see I couldn't do it either. But when I held the blade of grass it was as though my limbs, joints, and muscles had the experience of how to do this. I blew across the grass, on its edge, held tight between my thumbs. The noise it emitted was a low-pitched, crumbling noise.

"I want to try again!" she said.

"Let me watch you, maybe I can give you pointers," I told her. She picked another blade of grass and held it between her thumbs just as I had. She then blew a torrent of air against it. I cupped my hands around hers, situating the grass right in front of her mouth.

"Okay, do it again, but more softly this time." She tried it again, the air still torrent-like.

"More softly," I told her. This time, it worked, it wasn't the best whistle, but it was indeed a whistle.

She smiled, "I did it!" She threw the grass up in the air in celebration.

"Do you want me to push you on the merry-go-round?" I asked, standing up.

"Yes," she said, jumping on and grabbing on tight to one of the shiny metal bars. I ran around the merry-go-round as I too held on tight. After pulling at it a few times to get it really moving I jumped on. We spun until the merry-go-round was going infuriatingly slow. "Watch me jump off," she said. She jumped off and then I did.

"Mom!" she yelled, running toward Martha, who had just arrived.

Martha's son was with her. I didn't know much about Steven, except that he was Sydney's older brother, and he had answered the phone the first time I called Martha.

I said goodbye to Courtney and she wrapped her arms around my torso, leaving my arms floating in the air. It took me a second then I encircled her with my arms. After I let go of Courtney, Steven said to me, "My mom explained to me what you are doing with the story, and I wanted to offer to take you out to the place where Sydney fell."

This was unexpected but it seemed like a good idea.

"Yes, that would be helpful," I said, not completely sure I wanted to stand at the place of her death, but happy Sydney's family seemed to be supportive.

Twenty-six

Steven was to pick me up that Saturday morning, the same morning the neighbors had a yard sale. I was up well before Steven would get there and I walked over to the yard sale. It was a glorious collection of things that had cluttered their house, and were waiting to clutter the homes of those they would come to belong to. It was probably not making much money for them but I liked that it provided a project and a social outlet for the morning.

I walked around the items and picked up things one by one. I smelled candles, tried on jackets, and sifted through jewelry. I knelt in front of a bookshelf, and removed books one by one. The books were old, dusty, and rough around the edges. There were different heights and weights. I wondered if in one of them existed a world I would like to visit. I decided I needed a Crock-Pot, a box full of books, a variety of candles, and a new t-shirt. I conceded that 'need' was not an accurate word though, and I passed them all by.

I felt my face light up when I saw a collection of coffee mugs. There was a mug that looked similar to the emerald colored one from the stump. I picked it up and looked into it, examining it. It was deep, and I wondered how many hurried morning cups of coffee and late night cups of chamomile it had held. I looked at the couple holding the yard sale and wondered how it had been deemed unnecessary. It was marked at 25 cents and I decided it would be my purchase of the day. Out of the corner of my eye I saw a Mason jar. It was empty, holding only air. I did not know what I would do with it, but thought of my imaginary jar of chaos, and picked it up. I very much wanted that jar I held in my hands. It had a great deal of possibility. I took the two items up to the person who seemed to be in charge. I gave him a dollar, and put the change in the jar and closed the lid. It rattled a bit on the walk back over to the house. I found the noise unpleasant, given that I had not fully woken up.

When I got back home I rinsed out the mug and filled it with coffee, holding it gently and watching the ripples that formed when I blew on the steaming coffee. I contemplated the jar, wondering what it would hold.

Steven came to the door at 9:30 sharp. "Hello," I said with familiarity. I did not know Steven at all but had felt comfortable with him right away. We made our way out to his car and he opened the door for me. I climbed in, sinking into the seat.

Steven had stubble on his face and a football player's build. His hair was dark blond and cut short. He wore jeans and a maroon sweater. His car was lived in, or to put it less nicely, extremely messy. I liked that though. Messiness seemed more forgiving and more real than starched shirts and everything out of sight. This was despite the fact that my personal tendencies leaned toward neatness.

I told Steven about the yard sale and he told me about his job at an insurance agency. He was in sales, and it matched right away. I had a feeling he could be persuasive.

Then I asked, "Were you and Sydney close?"

"Yes and no," he said. We were three years apart and even though we were close growing up, when I graduated high school and moved out we drifted apart. She was still my little sister though and I would have done anything for her.

"What has it been like since she's been gone?" I asked.

"My parents are both devastated. I don't know what to say to them. Nothing I say seems to make any difference. I just don't get it, the way she was completely there, and now she's completely gone. I wonder where she is now. It doesn't seem possible that a person can just completely stop existing. I keep thinking she has to be somewhere."

"How have you been doing?"

"It's been hard. I won't lie, I've cried. I miss Sydney and it makes me sad there are so many people she will never meet, who will never see what an awesome person she was. It's hard to see my mom and dad so upset, and of course, Courtney. I feel especially bad for Courtney. She has closed up. She doesn't talk to me much lately. She and Sydney had a… special relationship. She's so young. I think it meant a lot to Courtney that you went to the park with her."

"I was glad to be there with her," I said with an appreciative gusto.

"She's so young," he said again.

Of course Steven knew Courtney was Sydney's daughter, but I didn't prod him about it and he didn't bring it up. The topic of Courtney brought a tension into the air. It was a tension that stopped us from going back to lighthearted conversation. He didn't seem to know what else to say and neither did I, so we sat in silence until we got to our destination.

As Steven parked the car he said, "It's confusing to get to where Sydney fell, but we've been out there a few times." I was a little concerned about the hike with my still broken toes but Steven reassured me, saying we could go slowly.

We were in the same general geographical area as the cove was. The surroundings were similar and I wondered how far away from the stump we were. The color scheme of the area was many shades of green and brown with large, gray rocks all over. I reached to touch leaves, tree trunks, branches, and rocks as we passed by them. I tried to grasp that the steps I was taking were the same steps Sydney had taken. We walked on a trail and then veered off. I was unsure of how Steven knew his way. He went slowly, for my sake. It was cold enough that I could see my breath in the air, but I felt warm, and enjoyed my surroundings.

We reached the cliff after a long while and stood at its edge, looking down. "Sydney fell from here," he said. As I looked down I tried to imagine what it must have felt like to be falling, knowing there was nothing you could do to save yourself. I wondered what thoughts had gone through Sydney's mind as she fell. Had she had time to think?

In a very convoluted manner we made our way to the bottom of the gorge. There was a big rock around which a rope was wound. It held a bloom of color to it.

"Did you put these flowers here?" I asked.

"Yes, it's Goldenrod," he said, "these are blooming everywhere right now. Courtney and I came out here together. I brought the rope and Courtney picked the flowers."

I had an impulse to sit on the rock but I wondered if that would be disrespectful, so I peered over the Goldenrod, examining it. It was a collection of tiny yellow flowers. Each flower had a voluminous center and the petals that came off the sides were tiny. Each flower was part of a string of flowers that formed rods.

"They're beautiful," I said, registering that I had seen them all over, both on the hike to the cliff and surrounding the cove.

The Goldenrod's deep yellow reminded me of the sun, and how it had been my companion on that first day when I woke up in the field. It seemed so long ago, that confusing day. I pulled my sleeves down over my hands. Instinctively I wanted to hide the scars on my wrists from Steven. I wanted him to see me beyond the scars, not through them. I kept the sleeves over my hands and crossed my arms. I looked at my feet, then up to his feet, then to his face.

"Thank you for bringing me out here Steven. Can I interview you at some point? Just ask some questions for Sydney's story?"

"Of course," he said, "Whatever I can do to help. Anytime."

Despite feeling a connection with Steven, I still did not think it was appropriate to ask about Courtney.

"I hope it helps to see where her last moments were," he said.

"It does, I'm glad we came out here. Seeing this place, where she fell, where she took her last breath, is powerful. I cannot imagine the terror she must have felt while falling."

"I know, it's hard not to think about that out here. I know she died quickly, and I'm grateful for that, that she didn't suffer too much."

"Steven, have you met Natalie, the friend who was out here with her the day she died?"

"None of us really know her. I met her at the hospital when she told us what happened, but then she disappeared. She wasn't at the funeral and I don't know anything about her. Natalie and Sydney worked together but they didn't meet until after college. She has been avoiding us as much as possible. I think she feels guilty, but it's not her fault."

"I'm going to be interviewing her. I called her, and she didn't seem too interested in being interviewed, but she agreed."

"Good," he said, "I hope that goes well. I have nothing against her. It was an accident. I wish she wasn't so withdrawn from us."

Steven and I walked back, and then he drove me home. I liked Steven, and reflecting on the outing as we drove, wondered if I had a brother, and if I did, would I ever know?

Twenty-seven

After Steven dropped me off I saw that the newspaper

was in the driveway. I picked it up and took the rubber band off

it. The front page of the paper had a story about the local school

board. I thought of how the binders never mentioned specific

schools or names. How was it I could have such a massive well

of information about myself and still not have any idea who I

was? I had not tried very hard to figure it out. Maybe the

information was there and maybe I did not want to know.

Maybe I was comfortable with life as it was. Maybe finding out

more would throw a wrench into everything.

The newspaper article about the fire did not have the

name of the paper, the date of the article, or the name of the

family. I could figure out the date though, couldn't I? I knew

when I had been born so all that was needed was to do the

math. The fire had happened nine years and three months after I

had been born.

Chances, I believed, were good that I lived somewhere

nearby. The field I woke up in was near where I ended up. If I was twenty-years-old that meant the fire had happened about eleven years ago. A fire that recent, one that destroyed a house, had to still be in the minds of people who had lived nearby, right? Somebody, if I was in fact from Carlton, would remember it. The potential accessibility of my identity through research of the newspaper article, could lead me anywhere.

I made the rest of the day busy and I let all my thoughts be absorbed by the busyness. I found myself wanting to be helpful that night, perhaps because I needed a break from my thoughts. I insisted on cleaning the entire kitchen by myself after dinner.

That night I watched the light from the moon flow down into the jar, that actual jar I could hold in my hands. I wanted to sleep, but could not close my eyes. I was mesmerized by the beauty of the moonlight flickering off the glass and metal lid. I remembered being in the hospital bed and filling the imaginary jar with the chaos that haunted me. I had thought I was going to deal with it later. But I had not dealt with it. It had stayed in that jar and I carried it still, every day, scared to open it. I was scared of what I would find and how I would deal with it. But what if I did open the metaphorical jar and let the chaos go? How much lighter would the load I carried become? What other things, I wondered, would I then be able to carry? I thought at first the jar from the yard sale simply made the connection for me. But then I realized the jar was the connection.

I looked at the clock. It was almost midnight. I took the jar and crept into the cold basement. I knew what I was looking for, I had seen it in passing. It was silver colored paint that looked like it had been in the basement a long time. I found it, took it outside, and sat on the damp grass. I took the lid off the paint can and off the yard sale jar.

I filled the jar halfway. I closed my eyes and thought of the jar from the hospital. I remembered what was in it, and imagined taking off its lid. That chaos rose up and I willed it to settle into the jar with the liquid silver. I looked into the jar, feeling the transfer had been successful. That jar from the hospital was no longer mine to carry. I put the lid on tight and turned the jar upside down, completely coating the inside with

279

silver. I wiped off the outside of the jar with my t-shirt and carried it up to my room. I put it in the same spot it had been in and it was alighted once again by the moon. There was another part of the plan, but it would come later. I wanted the silver painted jar to be in my view that night. I kept my eyes on the jar until sleep took me over, and then I slept soundly.

The next morning when I woke I had a new energy. I looked at the jar coated with paint and then I touched it with my index finger, pushing it an inch and feeling satisfied with my plan. I showered and dressed, mindfully, looking forward to the day. I took extra care in everything, taking seriously my outfit choice. I brushed my wet hair and then ran my hand over it, cool and smooth. I put lip gloss on and tied my shoes tight. I needed to be prepared for what the day may bring.

I quickly walked down the stairs and into the kitchen, as though I were on a mission. Even in the cold, it was like a spring day. Something as glorious as summer was on its way, I was going to find out who I was.

The library was bright, and large. There were microfilms of the Carlton paper and nearby papers. I started with the Carlton paper. There were no articles about the fire. Then I went to the papers of surrounding towns, nothing. Then I went to the papers of towns even further out. That was when I found it, the very article. The paper was the Lincolnton Citizen-Times. It was on page three. The timeline of the binders was accurate. I put the microfilms up and went to the computers.

I looked up Lincolnton, North Carolina on the internet and went to the 'Visit Lincolnton' page. It was the county seat of Starfield Country and seemed to have many attractions. I was eager to see everything and the site encouraged me to 'Plan a Trip to Lincolnton.' I had lived in Lincolnton when the fire happened. I had some kind of base there, and I wanted to find out more.

Twenty-eight

On the next Friday as I walked home from the diner I
was filled with anticipation about my meeting with Natalie that
would happen that evening. I thought about points I wanted to
hit, her background, how she knew Sydney, and how she was
doing now. I walked with my arms crossed and my purse
crossing from my shoulder to the opposite hip. Crossing my
arms brought an odd comfort, as though I were hugging myself,
as though I were fully within myself. When I got home I was
calm, I was not nervous at all, and I thought it was because my
day had so far been filled with work and walking. There was
something very nice about busyness, and work. My mind was
filled with enough that I did not have to worry.

Later that day when the doorbell rang I practically ran
to it, as best as you can run with three broken toes. I opened the
door and there was Natalie, I knew it was her. I shook her hand,
"Natalie? It's nice to meet you, I'm Ella. Please come in."

"It's nice to meet you too," she said.

Natalie's hair was long, brown, and looked messy, or maybe a little bohemian. Her eyes were dark and she was on the short side. I could see both sadness and joy in her face. I ushered Natalie to Cale's office. Cale's office had a chair behind the desk and two on the other side of the desk. Natalie and I sat in the two chairs on the other side of the desk. The chairs were the same and lent themselves to equality. I had thought sitting in the chair behind the desk would be too much like interviewer and interviewee.

"I'm glad you were able to make it, Natalie. Did you have any trouble finding the house?"

"No, no problem. Look, I don't want to talk about the accident," she said, directly and unflinchingly.

When Natalie said, "Look," there was something familiar about her. I couldn't place it, but it drew me to her and I wanted her to understand that I completely respected her wishes.

"Of course," I said, "I was just hoping to get to know you and if you want to we can talk about your friendship with Sydney."

"Okay," she said, looking a little friendlier.

I told Natalie about Cale and his obituary writing. I explained he was doing a collection of stories for his book, and I had been assigned to Sydney's story. I gave her no information about myself. I didn't tell her how it was I had come to work on Sydney's story, or why I was living at Cale's and Kristen's. She did not seem interested to know more and did not question me, which was a relief.

"Are you from Carlton?" I asked.

"No, I came here to go to Vance. I'm probably going to be moving soon."

"Oh," I said, not sure why, but realizing I was disappointed by the news she would be moving. "Where are you moving?"

"I don't know, but I know I don't want to be here. Every time I go to work I am reminded of the fact that Sydney is not there, and if we had not been hiking that day she would still be alive. I hate knowing that. I know people don't blame me, but I can't help thinking if it weren't for me she would still be alive."

"What is your job?" I asked, somewhat shocked I had never managed to find out what Sydney had done for work.

"I'm a bank teller and so was Sydney. I was finance major in college. I wasn't shooting to be a teller, but the job market is pretty competitive and the economy's not great. Sydney was not at all a finance type of person. She was just trying to figure out what her next step would be and the teller position was a good job that paid decently."

Natalie flipped her hair and sighed. This mannerism seemed familiar. Then I remembered something. I remembered being at school as a child, but it was not my school. I could see the figures of people, but not their faces. I was sitting on a desk and nobody seemed to notice me. I did not know where this memory had come from of what it meant. I shook my head, remembering Natalie was right there in front of me, and that I needed to pay attention.

"Are you ok?" she asked with concern, and I felt a longing for something. I did not know what. I made a concerted effort to focus on Natalie.

"Yes, yes. I'm fine, thanks." I felt my eyes blinking rapidly, and asked, "Do you have any brothers or sisters?"

"Yes, I have a brother, his name is Adrian. He's younger than me."

"Have you ever been to Lincolnton?" I asked, not having expected this to come out of my mouth.

"Sure, lots of times, why?" she responded.

"I'm going there with my friend, Sydney's friend, Kalyn. Would you like to come?" I did not know where that had come from. Kalyn and I had no plans to go to Lincolnton and certainly had no plans to ask Natalie to go there. I looked at Natalie and prayed she would say yes. There was something about her that felt right.

"Oh, well, maybe. When are you going?"

"Soon," I said out of nowhere. I did not know what I was doing.

"Is Kalyn… ok?" she asked. "What I mean by that is would it be comfortable, since she was a friend of Sydney's?"

"Oh yes, Kalyn is very friendly. I think you will get along very well."

"What are you planning on doing in Lincolnton?"

"Um… shop?" I said, more as a question.

"Well, that could be fun. Maybe, but it depends on when you go."

"This Saturday," I said. "I forgot earlier that we had decided on this Saturday." I wondered what Kalyn would think of this.

"Natalie hesitated and then said, "Well, ok, I could do that, but not until the afternoon, I have to work in the morning."

"Oh, perfect!" I said enthusiastically. "I have to work in the morning too. We were planning on leaving at 2:30." I was finding out these things at the same time as Natalie. I did not know what force had taken me over and why I was so insistent.

"Okay," she said. "It could be nice to get out of town for an afternoon."

"It will be great that you can go with us. Do you want to meet us here at 2:30?" I sure was hoping this would work out.

We hit the basic points I wanted to hit but I did not get very far with the conversation. After we decided to go to Lincolnton it was mostly inconsequential small talk, but it helped build our relationship. Despite Natalie's guardedness I did indeed feel drawn to her. After she left I suddenly realized it was Friday and though we had never referred to Saturday as 'tomorrow,' I had just made plans to go to Lincolnton with Natalie and Kalyn the next day. I supposed that Natalie had known Saturday was the next day.

I immediately called Kalyn. Luckily we had become close enough that the situation was semi-acceptable. I told her the whole situation, having no idea if she would be willing and able to go to Lincolnton at 2:30 the next day... and if she could drive. I apologized but it did not seem to bother her. She said she would love to come, and yes, she could drive. Kalyn said she looked forward to meeting her and that she would come over the next day at 2:30. The plans were set and Kalyn, Natalie, and I would be headed to Lincolnton the next day.

The next day I did what was becoming my usual morning walk and work routine and got home at about 2:00. I quickly took a shower and changed and was coming downstairs when the doorbell rang. It was Natalie and when I saw her my breath caught. There was something so familiar about her. Kalyn came shortly afterwards and I introduced them to each other. They were in keeping with how I knew them, Kalyn was open and friendly and Natalie was guarded. No mention was made of Sydney and no one would have guessed the odd circumstances of how we all knew each other.

Twenty-nine

The car ride to Lincolnton was to take an hour. I sat in the front with Kalyn and Natalie sat in the back. This made for a little bit of a self-conscious (for me) ride since neither Kalyn nor I really knew Natalie. I didn't want to exclude her. I was anxious and half-turned around most of the ride, trying to talk to both Natalie and Kalyn. I still did not know what particular thing drew me to Natalie but I was happy to spend time with her under the guise of shopping. Unlike Carlton, which was in the foothills, Lincolnton was in the mountains and we steadily went uphill.

We saw some mountain vistas on the way up there but they were distant and did not seem real. When we got into the mountains we saw the heaps of mountains up close. I could not remember ever being that near mountains. They were packed with trees and somehow this seemed unusual. I had imagined the mountains as vast creatures of breathtaking beauty. Up close, while still lovely, they were more real. Had they been human I would have said they were more human. Then we reached an overlook, and we stopped. I saw in that place, where mountains were as far as I could see, they were indeed vast creatures of breathtaking beauty. For a moment, I felt assurance that all was right in the world. While the moment was an eye blink, it was one that had definitely existed. Although I couldn't remember it, I knew I had seen that view before. It was not so much that it looked familiar, but it felt familiar, in the same way Natalie felt familiar.

When we got back into Kalyn's car and she tried to turn it on it sputtered some, but did not start. It wasn't the battery, Kalyn believed, she had just gotten a new one, but there was no one at the overlook to jump the car and see. She had plenty of gas.

We were ten miles from Lincolnton and Kalyn had just enough cell service to look up a garage that could come out. She called and they told us they would be there in an hour. A minivan had pulled into the overlook and a family piled out. They asked if I could take a picture of them and I obliged. As we waited my mind ran wild with the beauty of the mountains.

The minivan had long since left when a tow truck pulled in to us.

The man looked like he worked in a garage and looked like he knew what he was doing. He popped the hood and tried jumping the car, but it wasn't the battery. He looked around under the hood a bit and said he would have to tow it back to their garage to see what was wrong. The three of us crowded into the front of his pickup and he towed the car to the garage, about twenty minutes away, in Lincolnton.

When we got there he told us he could get to it the next afternoon. They had several cars in front of us.

"Tomorrow afternoon?" Kalyn questioned.

"Yep, tomorrow, can't get to it today."

"But... but... we don't live here. Is there any way you can get to it today?"

"You can have it towed to another garage. I can give you some numbers."

"Yes, if you could," Kalyn said tensely.

Kalyn made some calls and found a garage that might be able to work on it that day, but they'd have to take a look at it, and there was no guarantee. Natalie, much to my surprise, made an intriguing proposition.

"What if we spent the night here? I don't work tomorrow. I don't know what you both have going on, but it could be fun. We could split a hotel room." Given Natalie's guardedness, she was the last of the three of us that I thought would have suggested that. I looked at Kalyn but could not read her reaction.

"That could be a problem," I said, "I don't have enough money to split a hotel room." I had $18 of tip money with me. I suddenly realized it was ridiculous that I had said we were going shopping.

"I don't have extra money either, Kalyn said, "I don't even know how much it is going to cost to have my car fixed."

"If it doesn't make you uncomfortable, I would be happy to pay if we can find somewhere that's not too much, I just got my paycheck," Natalie said. It was then I saw that

Natalie, while guarded, had a great deal of generosity when something cracked the surface, and it saw it was an illusion that guardedness meant inaccessibility.

Kalyn and I both protested, but Natalie insisted and really, the scenario made sense. The only other option I could think of were to get the car towed back to Carlton and for Kalyn come back the next day. Though this was a possible option, spending the night was just as viable, if not more so. The next day was Sunday, so none of us were in a rush to get back. It only seemed right to protest Natalie paying for all of us, and so we did once more. I was rooting for Natalie to keep offering though, and she did, so we decided to stay the night.

"Okay," Kalyn told the man who had picked us up, "We will stay overnight, is there a hotel nearby?"

"There's one about four miles or so from here. Do you need a ride?"

"Please, if you could," Kalyn said.

After checking into the hotel we wandered around nearby stores and restaurants. Luckily there were plenty near the hotel. We went into a drug store and bought toiletries we would need. We walked past the business district into a more residential area and that is when we saw the school. It was an elementary school and I was sure I had seen it before.

I saw the playground and had a significant memory. I remembered running on that very playground. Then I remembered the cafeteria, and then being dropped off in front of the school by a woman whose face I could not see.

We walked back into the business district and split a pizza at a restaurant. When we went back to the hotel it was dark. We got a double room with a cot. We didn't talk much and went to bed early. The next morning after partaking in the continental breakfast Kalyn called the garage, but they didn't open until noon because it was Sunday. We went back to our room until check-out time at 11:00 and then walked around the business district again. I asked if we could go back to the school, and we did. We sat on the playground equipment and in the bright morning light I knew I was home. I knew Lincolnton was my home.

As we sat there I talked. The things I was saying were partly known by Kalyn, but not at all by Natalie. I talked about losing my memory, the cove, and the article about the fire. I told them the real reason I had wanted to come to Lincolnton was because I had found out the article about the fire was from the Lincolnton paper. I told them I was sure I had gone to this school. Natalie didn't seem to believe me, but I could accept that. I was glad I had told her.

We were there until 12:30 and Kalyn called the garage. They said they would have it fixed by 4. We decided to get lunch and then go to a movie. When we walked out of the movie theater I heard someone say my name.

"Ella, hi, how are you?" I looked at this unfamiliar person. "I haven't seen you in years. So you're back? I did not hear you were back. Are you doing okay? I bet your parents are happy."

I was silent. This was somebody who knew who I was. I didn't know how to react.

"Have you seen my parents lately?"

"Not lately, just in the news."

"In the news? For what?"

"He gave me an odd look. Because you were missing…"

"Right, of course," I said, pretending that I already knew this. I looked at his torso, unable to make eye contact. He worked there. He was wearing a blue polo shirt with the movie theater's small logo in the upper left part of the chest. I didn't know what to do, but I knew what my trigger response was. This was my chance, and I was going to go for it.

"To be quite honest," I said after a long pause, "I don't know who I am or who my parents are. Can you help me?" It was a bold question to ask.

He looked at me, dumbfounded.

"You're Ella Abner. We went to high school together."

"Right, of course, never mind." I suddenly felt very vulnerable. Ella Abner. "It was good to see you. See you later."

I was rigid. This was really happening. I looked at Kalyn and Natalie.

"I'm looking up 'Abner,'" Kalyn said, pulling out her phone. "Here it is, call this number." She handed me the phone and I realized it was already ringing. A woman answer and I quietly said "hi."

"Ella, is that you? Ella? Ella?" I was quiet.

"Are you there? Oh my God. Ella?" Time stopped. Who was this woman? But I knew, it was my mother. I knew that voice. The voice was desperate. I couldn't think and I couldn't breathe. I wanted time to hurry up and start again, because that place I was in felt too overwhelming to talk in. I cheered myself on. 'Just say hello,' I thought. 'Just hello,' and then I did, in a whisper.

"Hello," I said, more loudly this time. "This is Ella." The woman was screaming and I was saying nothing. Kalyn grabbed the phone from me.

"Hello," she said, "Mrs. Abner?" I could hear a muffled voice on the other end of the line. I clearly heard the word 'daughter.'

"Yes," Kalyn said, "She's right here."

A pause, and then from Kalyn, "We're at the movie theater in Lincolnton."

Another pause, and then from Kalyn, "We'll wait for you here."

I felt paralyzed. I looked at Natalie's wide eyes and then turned and went to sit down.

Kalyn hung up the phone and sat down next to me. "She said you're her daughter, and you have been missing."

We sat in silence and then after fifteen minutes a couple came in, hurried and hysterical.

"Ella!" the woman said, the same voice I had heard over the phone. I stood up and she wrapped me in her arms. There was a man there, and there were tears falling from his eyes. He hugged me next. Then the woman hugged me again.

"I'm sorry," I said, "I'm not totally sure who you are." I knew this was my mother and father, but at the same time I did not clearly remember them, and a big part of them seemed like strangers. I wilted as they hugged me.

"We've been searching for you. Have you been right here in Lincolnton this whole time?"

Silence.

"You really don't remember us, my girl?" I heard grief carry her words. "I'm your mom and this is your dad," she said, touching his shoulder.

"No," I said, jumping back to the question of if I'd been in Lincolnton the whole time. "I've been living in Carlton. But I lost my memory. I didn't know who I was. One day I just woke up in a field, and that was two months ago. I have had some memories come back... but I didn't know who I was."

I didn't know what to do or where to go from there. So I went to their home, and Kalyn and Natalie came too. 'Mom' called the police station and told them that her daughter Ella was back. The police were going to come over.

I told them about the field, the hospital, and Cale and Kristen. I left most things out though. They told me I had been missing for almost two months. That I had just disappeared upon my release from the hospital in Jackson, the town neighboring Carlton. I saw pictures of myself in their house. I was confused and upset though, and told them I couldn't stay there, that I needed to go home.

The police said they needed me to stay. That they needed me to come to the station the next day. I could hardly look at the desperation in the woman's eyes, and wanted to escape. So I stayed and the police took Kalyn and Natalie to the garage where Kalyn's car was. I called Cale and told him what had happened. Right after the police left I told them I was tired. I wanted physical refuge, in the form of an empty bedroom. It was all overwhelming.

"Of course," the woman said. "I suppose you don't remember where your room is?"

"No."

"Let me show her," the man said. I followed him to another part of the house. "It's right here," he said, opening the door. "Are you hungry? Do you need anything?"

I was hungry and sure there were things I needed, but I denied both.

The woman came to the door, "Let me fix you some dinner."

"No, thanks."

"Let me get you a towel and you can take a shower. You still have some clothes here, they're in the dresser and closet."

"Okay," I said, intensely wanting to be by myself. She brought a towel and washcloth and I closed the door behind her. I sat on the floor and leaned against the bed. I looked around me. I saw picture frames that had me in them, old and worn stuffed animals, and the mass variety of things that make up a person's childhood bedroom.

I got up and went to the bathroom, taking a long shower. I found pajamas in the dresser and put them on and sat on the bed.

I heard a knock on the door, it was the woman, "Ella, are you doing okay? Can I come in?"

I didn't say anything and saw the door open up a crack.

"Ella, I'm sorry, it's just I can't believe you're back. Won't you please come out and have some dinner?"

I had to admit that I was hungry. "Okay," I said.

I followed her to the kitchen and sat down at the kitchen table.

"What do you want? I'll make you anything."

"It doesn't matter."

"Oh Ella, come on, anything you want."

"Cereal would be fine."

"Ella, no, let me make you a real meal."

"Anything's fine," I said.

"How about taco salad? That's what we had for dinner."

"Sure, that sounds great." She got busy preparing the taco salad, and there was a plate in front of me in minutes. As I ate she sat across from me and stared at me.

"So," I said, "Well, first of all, please don't stare at me. It's making me nervous."

"Oh, I'm sorry dear."

"So, I started again, do I have any brothers or sisters?"

"No, you're an only child. We did not think we would be able to have children, we were thrilled to have you."

I thought about the things I had found out about in the binders, but decided not to ask her about any of them.

Thirty

The next morning, after waking up, as I lay in bed, I remembered. Corey had died in a car accident. It had been a rainy night. Although he had been going the speed limit, it was too fast for the conditions. I had buried him in the back of my mind and finding that out brought him back. The feeling I had the day I cut my wrists, I suddenly remembered vividly. It was the same as when I fell down the stairs, the same consuming despair.

It hadn't been that I wanted to take my life, just like with the stairs, it had been that I wanted the pain and choas to end, that it felt far too overwhelming to know how to possibly cope with it. That day, those months ago, I felt weak and sad. And it wasn't just Corey, it wasn't just what happened. It was the sense that I was alone, that I was too vulnerable, that I was too weak. It was the understanding I had been damaged, and could never be as good as I once had been. There was a cap on my goodness, a ceiling. Goodness was a place I could see but a place it would never have been possible to reach. Corey's death had brought all these feelings to the surface.

I had broken a mirror, feeling already damned, bring on seven more years of bad luck. Nobody found me. The carpet was soaked in blood and it was me who picked up the phone.

"911, what's your emergency?" she asked.

"I… I made a mistake. I didn't mean to do this. I broke a mirror and then used it to cut my wrists. I'm sorry, I just did it. I didn't realize it would hurt me." I knew that did not make sense, that I had not realized it would hurt me. How could I not know it would hurt me? I had been in a singular place though, all I saw was my pain.

I was still conscious when the ambulance came, but I was woozy, not really all there. I barely remembered the ambulance ride, and I didn't remember much after that. I remembered the ICU and the few people who came to visit me. I remembered asking each person who came, "Can you hold my hand?"

All that was with me was feeling myself in my body. Feeling myself fully. Feeling the sensation of my body in the bed, the hospital gown, the socks on my feet, the sheet over me, the pillow under my head, the burning in my wrists. The feeling of being nothing more than a body, scared I didn't have a soul. Then the IV was gone and I was in the car with my mother, she was taking me to a different hospital, 45 minutes away.

I did remember the next hospital. I remember being told I had to go, that I had no choice, I was being committed. I protested, but weakly.

The crisis worker had been looking for a placement, 'looking for a bed,' was how she put it. She found one and I went there, bandages on my wrists.

It was midnight when we got there and we rang a doorbell. A man opened the door. I said goodbye to my mom and the man brought me in. He ran a metal detector over me. It gave off a high pitched wail when it reached my feet.

"It's just the floor," he said, kindly.

I went through the double doors onto the unit. The doors were old, the whole building was old. I felt the blood drain out of my face as I took a step over the threshold. It was surreal to me. The adrenaline in my body was building up and I felt ready to sprint. I stood still but felt frantic. They took my purse and my bag.

"We will give you back what you are allowed to have."

I was taken to an exam room.

"We have to do a skin assessment," she said. "Take off your top." I took it off. "Take off your bra." I slowly reached to the clasp on my back and unhooked it, and took off my bra.

"Put your arms out and turn in a circle." I turned in a slow circle, topless.

"No scars? No tattoos?"

"No," I said.

"Put this on," she said, handing me a hospital gown. I put it on.

"Take off your jeans." I took off my jeans. "And your socks and underwear." I slid my underwear off and lifted my foot up with them hooked over my foot. I picked them up and then took off my socks, laying it all beside my feet.

"Lift up your gown and turn in a circle." I did so.

"No scars? No tattoos?"

"No," I said.

She gave me another gown. "You can wear this as a robe." I let the gown fall around me and put the other gown on. It concealed the open gap in the back. She told me I could put my socks and underwear back on.

"You can sit down."

I sat in the plastic chair. "Do you hear voices?" she asked. "No, of course not," I said. I was terrified. "What medications do you take?" "None. There's nothing wrong with me, I just made a mistake." "Mmm hmm" she said, dismissively. "Can't a person make a mistake every once in a while?" She didn't respond, but just went on to ask more questions to which nearly ever answer was "no."

"You can leave," she said, putting gloves on and picking up my clothes, "we will wash these and give them back

to you tomorrow. Except your bra. Underwire. Are you
hungry?"

"Yes."

She took me to another room and brought me a
styrofoam to-go box. It had a ham and cheese sandwich in it,
plus a bag of chips and a plastic cup of applesauce. She did not
offer me anything to drink. I hadn't eaten in many hours, and
appreciated the meal.

There were many people awake, in the common room,
but none of the other patients looked at me or talked to me.

"You can go to bed if you want," the nurse told me. I
did not see a trash can so I closed the styrofoam container and
left it on the table, too tired and intimidated to ask where the
trash was. I looked down at my feet as I stood up. The socks
had grips on them, presumably to keep me from slipping, my
shoes had been taken away. She pointed to my room. There
were two beds in the room but it was empty. I could see I had a
roommate though, one of the beds was unmade. I closed the
door behind me, turned off the light, and fell into bed. The next

thing I knew I was in a haze of the remnant of dreams and the room was filled with artificial light, florescent..

"We need to take your blood pressure," the nurse said. I sleepily went out into the hallway and walked toward the front desk with her. "Sit here."

I sat in the plastic chair and a blood pressure cuff was wrapped around my arm and a thermometer stuck in my mouth. Then the machine started beeping and the blood pressure cuff was taken off and the thermometer taken out.

"You can go back to sleep." I looked at the clock over the nurses' station, it said 5:30.

The next five days passed so slowly it seemed like weeks went by. One afternoon I looked at the clock, shocked that it was only 3:00 pm but then I realized I had transposed the numbers. It was only 12:15 pm. A wave of dread and boredom passed through me when I realized that. I had very little human interaction in the hospital. I planned to stay with a long-time friend in Carlton for a few days after I got out. They wanted to know where I was going so I told them Gracie and that she was in Carlton. When I told my parents this I told them as if I had already talked to my friend. I had not, but was sure it would work out fine. I knew my friend would have no problem with this because she was that kind of friend. My parents were upset I didn't want to go with them, but I just couldn't face them.

When I called my friend she did not answer and so I didn't talk to her at all while I was in the hospital. The day before I left I told the Social Worker about my plans to stay with my friend. I did not share that I had not actually talked to her. I was thinking about alternate plans in my mind, not wanting to show up unannounced, when she said, "we can cab you."

"Oh, okay. What does that mean?" I asked.

"We will call you a cab, it will be covered." I meant to protest, to say I had not been in touch with her, that I did not want to show up unannounced, but she seemed to have already made the decision. I just went with it.

When I got into the cab the next day, I gave him my friend's address, still very hesitant about showing up unannounced. She lived a county over in the country and when we pulled up and I got out I realized she was not there. I knocked on her door anyway and looked in the windows. It was empty and I decided to put my bags into her cellar where they would be safe. I walked out behind her house, across a stream, and up and over a hill. I saw a vast field that sloped down and a forest in the distance. I began running across the field, feeling the swift air and freedom. Then I fell, it was as if I had been struck by lightning. When I woke up I remembered nothing.

Sydney

Thirty-one

The day Sydney fell off the cliff and died, Natalie was

led to the cove by a Buttonquail, a bird native to Australia. The

bird was not really a bird. In fact, it was a man, and his name

was Jeremy. Jeremy had gone to the Holding Place five years

earlier, when he was 24, after he died of a rare kind of bone

cancer. When he was alive, Jeremy studied birds. He liked the

way they were free. When he was seven he had been given a

pair of binoculars for his birthday. His parents sensed his

interest and with the binoculars his fascination with birds took

off. He had grown up in South Australia, and as a child and

adult he was always on the hunt for native birds of the region.

His favorite was the Buttonquail, in part because he liked its

name. That was the bird he had chosen to be when he flew.

Because he had assignments all over the world, he was

often quite out of place as a Buttonquail. However, humans

have the remarkable and sometimes unfortunate ability to

rationalize anything. When someone sensed he was out of

place, they rarely took it further, generally accepting it and moving on.

Jeremy had many experiences with the people on Earth in his quest to fulfill his task. Once, Jeremy was in the Philippines and he settled on a hospital ledge. He was there constantly for days. There was inside the room a boy who was dying. Understandably his parents were distraught, and even more so because their daughter was not there to be with her brother in his last days.

After Jeremy had been there consistently for four days, and only the father and son were in the room, the father started to feel the peace that Jeremy's presence was meant to give him. Jeremy's presence had a dual purpose though. It was meant that this bird, beautiful and out of the ordinary, would trigger this man to call his estranged daughter, so she could see her brother in the final days of his life. Growing up she had a bird she kept. She had long-nurtured it and it had been a part of their family. This would be the last chance she had to see her brother. The man did reach out to her daughter, and told her how the bird had become their constant companion. He told her how it made him think of her childhood, and how he loved her. She was touched by the way he connected it to her, and made it to see her brother before he died.

Jeremy's task in the Holding Place was just that, connection. When he was given the task he was given abilities that were unique and suited toward his task. When each person in the Holding Place is given a task they were given special abilities to help them achieve their task. One of the abilities he was given was to go to Earth in human or bird form. The day Natalie followed him after Sydney's death he was fully present and he flew through the woods with her following him.

The wind had whipped his body and he would momentarily close his eyes, feeling, it seemed, the most free a being could possibly feel. He loved flying fast, letting the sensation overtake him, and flying slowly, looking at everything around him, taking in the gentleness of the world. He could sit on the shoulders of animals or humans. He could get very close to the ground or high in the sky. Either way he was viewing the world through unique lenses. He flew around the Holding Place and around Earth. He could clearly see that at a very high point they looked quite similar. As he would descend to each of them their realities became clearer, and he saw how different they were. But from the highest heights, they had dynamic beauty, both. It was the Earth's beauty that was sometimes hard to see when he was very close to the surface.

When Sydney reached the Holding Place, Jeremy sought her out. He saw her body when he went to Earth, but at that point Sydney had already been taken to the Holding Place. He knew what she would be experiencing, the shock of change and the joy and grief of being in the Holding Place instead of on Earth. She would be experiencing the yearning for loved ones on Earth, but looking forward to new possibilities too.

Jeremy went to the house of her expanded family. She was with those who loved her and who had gone before her. Her house reached above the clouds and she lived near the top of the house. Her view of the Holding Place was one Jeremy had seen often as he flew. When he knocked at the front door a distant relative of Sydney's gruffly answered.

"Hello," Jeremy said, "I'm looking for Sydney, she is new here." The relative, though gruff, had kind eyes. Jeremy easily accepted that while everyone presented themselves differently, everyone also had good within them. Beyond the pain and difficulty that had a hand in shaping them on Earth, there was good underneath it all.

"Sure, I'll get her," he said, scowling.

"Thank you sir," Jeremy answered.

Sydney looked lost as she descended the stairs. She was still adjusting and a task had not yet been given to her.

"Hi," she said, with curiosity.

"Hi Sydney, my name is Jeremy. I saw you on Earth, after you died, and I wanted to meet you."

They went to a porch swing that hung high in the sky, just below the clouds. It was connected to the house and the height made Sydney nervous, not only because she could fall, but because she had died from a fall. Jeremy told her if she managed to fall she would be caught by air. This eased her fear, and she knew she had instinctively known this already. She sat there with him, swinging her feet and looking at all that lay below.

Sydney talked about the newness of it all, and how she was sad for those on Earth who grieved her. She talked about her adjustment and told him of the many different people in her expanded family, and their different tasks. She was taking it all in, a little bit at a time. It was amazing to her there were people who already knew her. She marveled at the way all worked together to meet each other's needs. She had immediately felt absorbed into the community of the Holding Place. Though she felt lost, it was only because the depth of the newness was immense.

Jeremy talked passionately about what it was like to fly and told her of flying through the woods to take Natalie to the cove. He told her that in the beginning he had chosen to be a Buttonquail, a bird that was beautiful but not flashy. That it was native to his homeland of Australia, a place he loved, missed,

and sometimes visited. His accent was rich, and Sydney loved
it.

Jeremy and Sydney's friendship was a rapid happening.
That day, as Sydney was drawn to Jeremy's passion for flying,
Jeremy was equally drawn to the way Sydney seemed to be free
on her own. Sydney found in Jeremy someone who listened,
and when her words were securely in his ears, they were no
longer hers to bear alone. Jeremy saw in Sydney someone
lovely and interesting, someone whose abrupt ending would not
lessen the potential she had to touch the world. They talked
until it grew dark and the temperature cooled. When they
parted, they each felt they had known each other for many
years.

Sydney received her task shortly, and like the tasks
which many in the Holding Place held, it was a task that was
jointed with Earth. Unlike many though, she would pass
through the barrier of the Holding Place and Earth continually.
Her task would lead her to pass back and forth through the two
the same way a person's forearm lifted up and down, bending

at the elbow. Sydney would be assigned people on Earth, ones who were fragile, ones who struggled, and ones who were at risk, and help keep them from breaking. To help keep the world from breaking them open and letting darkness spill into them.

Most people who live in the world have an exterior which may be wounded, bent, and bruised, but the skin of their psyches does not open, and their bones do not break badly enough to pierce that skin. These people may even fracture, but they are fractures that heal. There are some people, the ones whose skin opens, whose bones will only heal in a way that will leave them deformed, that were the ones Sydney would be assigned to. Even with her presence there were no guarantees, Sydney could only do her best.

She would do her best though, and her best would be very good, and that was why she had been given the task. Ultimately only a person can prevent themselves from breaking. Still though, there was much she could do. She had a good knowledge of tools and an understanding of humans that would be a great asset in this area. It was a hard job, to watch a person fracture, and let them, but to stop it short of a break.

A fracture is not a bad thing, and not something that needs to be prevented. It is human nature to fracture, and something that is even good for people. A fracture gives enough pain and understanding to help a person have the capability for dealing with difficult aspects of life. The problem though, and this is something Sydney would come to learn well, is that some people, for whatever reason, are hurt beyond fractures. It was those specific people that Sydney focused on, the fragile, struggling, those at risk in whatever way. Some may be more sensitive to the despair of the world and some may have received something to deal with that nobody could properly deal with. Sydney would struggle against situations where she felt helpless, but no one but the person them self can prevent a total break.

Thirty-two

The first assignment was no coincidence. The first person assigned to Sydney was Ella. Had Sydney not died, the perfect opportunity for Sydney's friend and Somer's sister, Natalie, to visit the Holding Place would not have existed. Had Sydney not died, Somer would not have had that opportunity to join with the other part of her, Ella, on Earth, and Ella wouldn't have lost her memory. Ella and Somer, while they were indeed delicate people on their own, had experienced such a degree of trauma when they collided into one another, they became at risk of breaking. It was such a beautiful thing, the way a miracle had wrought them together, but it would not have been worth it if that led to Ella's destruction.

The hardest part of being in the Holding Place for Sydney was not that she was no longer with her loved ones. It was hard knowing they grieved for her and knowing there was nothing she could do about it. If only she could let them know her life was not over. If only she could protect them from the pain of her death. If only she could hold Courtney and let her know it was not the end. She wanted to tell those on Earth even though they could not pick up the phone and talk to her, she was still there, and she still loved them.

Many times, Somer, while she lived in the Holding Place, had hovered around her Earth family, wanting to feel their presence, wanting to be near them. This was tempting for Sydney, too. Sydney did, a few times, visit her family on Earth, visiting Courtney and the others. But the pain in Courtney, her beloved daughter, was palpable, and her uselessness regarding this felt absolute. She could see Courtney's smile and her tears but there was nothing she could do to let Courtney know she was there.

When she was alive Sydney had told Courtney, without really meaning to, that she was not her sister, she was her mother. Sydney had always loved Courtney like a mother would love a child. It was unconditional and complete. She took joy in Courtney's life and when she struggled with something it broke her heart. If she could have gone back in time she would have never agreed to have Courtney raised by her mom, to have Courtney think they were sisters. She had been a scared teenager though, and wanted the best for Courtney, even before she was born. Maybe she did make the right choice for Courtney, but oh, how she wished she could have been a real mom to her.

After the first few times, Sydney did not visit anymore. She felt like her family's pain was her fault and though it simply showed they had loved her, she could not bear that she had caused them so much pain.

When Sydney was assigned to Ella she was also given background information. She was told how Somer died shortly after birth and the way her soul was splintered at the moment of her death. That Somer grew up in the Holding Place and Ella grew up on Earth. It was explained that a miracle splintered them at birth and merged them back together. The merging was traumatic and Ella, who was also Somer, woke up with no memory afterward. Sydney was told that Ella was born with a sensitive bent but had not been at risk for breaking until they were merged. She had the capacity for great joy, but also, great pain.

Like Jeremy was given the gift of flying, Sydney was given gifts too. She could touch the Earth enough to alter small things, things that would put helpful opportunities in Ella's path. She had the gift of influence, for things that would help Ella and her other assignments. Her hand on Earth would never be seen by anyone living there, but small things she influenced had the potential to make a real difference to Ella.

Sydney said to Jeremy out of frustration after being given her task, "This seems like a huge responsibility, too big. How can I be expected to save someone?"

"You do have a great responsibility set before you, Sydney. I believe you may be misreading it a bit. You are right, you cannot save anyone, nobody but a person's own self has that power. But you can put things in their path to help them do that. That is actually a basic tenant of existence. To help other people help themselves. Your task is special though. You are able to genuinely alter the world, like a human living on Earth

327

would. But you have to be more intentional than if you were human. Your sole duty is to alter the world in small but powerful and positive ways, to make things better for humans. Our tasks are given to us in accordance to our abilities, and not beyond that. When it is hard you can talk to me, whenever you want. I think you should visit the library, it is a great library, and it is in a castle."

Jeremy told her for every person living on Earth there was a room in the library filled with information about them. There were people whose task it was to follow a person on Earth, and record information about them. Even the loneliest people and those who lived solitary lives needed a witness to their life. Most of the time, those with this task did not follow a person for life, but it was an assignment that was shared. Most people were not in the Holding Place long enough to follow a whole life. Most lives were not short enough to be followed completely by one person. The person with this assignment could choose to check on them once a day or a few times a day. It varied with the person in the Holding Place, what their style

328

and personality was. Those who were given this task tended to be meticulous to varying degrees. Every person's room had a different feel to it. This recording of a person's life made it easy to reference occurrences after the fact. For someone whose task it was to keep a person from breaking, they could reference something from the past in the room of their life.

The towering castle of a library served all of the Holding Place. People in any part of the Holding Place could reach it. It was like a town square, on a very large scale. It expanded to hold anything a person wanted to find. It was swarmed with people of varying nationalities and languages. In the library Sydney found she could understand any language a person spoke. Spending time there made her understand no matter what a person looked like, what race, nationality, or age they were, they were all the same. All of their eyes held a pupil, iris, and were embraced and surrounded by white. All of their eyes sat underneath lashes and lids.

In the time Sydney spent in the library she encountered many people. Deep into the eyes of each person she encountered, she saw lives she knew nothing about. She heard their voices though, and their words made sense, no matter the language they spoke.

That first time she went into the library she was awestruck. In the main area, the town square section, so to speak, she saw no walls, except for the wall at the door she came in. The area seemed endlessly big.

There were conversations going on everywhere. Scattered around were people reading newspapers, Earthly papers that seemed to be in all different languages. Sydney understood the titles that stood out on each paper, even though many were not in English.

There was a giant circulation desk that looked like a massive line of bank tellers. She walked up to one of the librarians and asked if she could see Ella Abner's room. She gave Ella's place of birth and birthday. Sydney was told she would need to fill out a form and submit it. A decision would be made within one to two days if she would be granted access to the room. The librarian explained these were very private rooms. It would need to be determined what her motives were and how she would use the information. They would determine if she was allowed at all and if there would be any limitations to her access.

Sydney filled out a short form, unsure of how they would determine these things, but not doubting they would be able to. She was also unsure of how they would contact her, since they did not ask for any contact information, but she was confident they had a system.

After submitting the form Sydney wandered around the library. Were it truly a castle then she would have been in the ballroom, and a giant one at that. The floors were marble and the ceiling was tall and from the gold ceilings hung chandeliers. At even intervals in the room were columns, as if they held up the ceiling. Sydney imagined wearing a beautiful, flowing dress, perhaps with a fitted, sparking bodice and a full skirt. Perhaps sky blue with a violet sash around her waist. Perhaps her hair was up and filled with pearls. Perhaps she wore silver slippers, ones that allowed her to twirl. She imagined a room filled with music and dancing. She closed her eyes and imagined twirling. Perhaps.

She continued to walk around, looking at the large variety of people. In addition to people reading newspapers there were also people reading books and children being read to. Most people were in conversation though.

As she kept walking she reached a section of books. She had a feeling the book section went on unendingly. There were many more librarians in this part and she asked one of them what books were in the library. Sydney was told every book that had ever been written, published or unpublished, on Earth or in the Holding Place, was included. The librarian told her she needed a library card to check a book out. She filled out another short form and was told she could begin checking out books. There was no actual card. Somehow, apparently, the fact she had filled out the form would somehow shine through. She browsed the shelves and realized the books were in different languages, but she could understand what they all said. Sydney wondered how she would ever pick out a book.

The aisle she was on was long and deserted. She ran down it for over a minute and then stopped and faced one of the shelves. She put her left hand over her eyes and with her right index finger she pointed to a book. She opened her eyes and pulled the book she was pointing to off the shelf. She took the book without really looking at it and checked it out. She was asked to turn it in when she was done with it.

Sydney walked all the way back to the library's front door. She sat down on an empty place on the steps that seemed boundless on either side. There were people sitting everywhere, the sun shining on them. She looked at the book then, it was a murder mystery written in 1928. It was written in an Asian language and instead of letters she saw symbols, but she understood them. She sat down on the steps and read the first chapter, people coming and going all around her. She was surrounded and by herself, in the best way possible.

The next morning Sydney treasured, as she always did. She was happy the day before was completed and closed out and understood the new day held the most strength it would, right at that moment of waking. That before uttering the first word, anything at all could be.

Sydney opened the door to the front porch and stepped out, taking in the dew on the grass. It was as though the mist coming from the grass were made of a violinist playing invigorating, passionate music. It was a new day, and the sun would soon douse her. In the Holding Place you could look straight at the sun and it wouldn't hurt your eyes. No matter how long its rays hit your skin, it never burned.

After stepping onto the porch and taking in the dew, Sydney turned to go back inside, to prepare for the day. She had not noticed it before, though she must have stepped over it. She bent down and picked up the small envelope. Her name was written on the creamy, white front. When she turned it over she saw it was sealed and stamped in rich black ink. The stamp had no words, but was the image of an open book. Again, she felt the sense of possibility that was continually in the air she breathed.

Sydney could feel something sturdy inside the envelope. There was a thin, rounded part of it which connected two differently shaped ends. Sydney opened the envelope and pulled out a key. The key was a bronze color and shiny, as though it had never been used before. There was nothing else with it but she supposed it was a key to Ella's room. It was a wondrous moment for Sydney. The music that had seemed to drift off the grass in the dew that morning became even more real, and she imagined herself on the front row of a symphony.

Sydney could not wait to step into Ella's room. Around her neck Sydney had a necklace that was made by a craftsman in the Holding Place. It had been given to her after she admired it around the artist's neck. In exchange she helped clean the studio he worked out of. She also spent time with a young boy who spent hours at a time in the studio. It had seemed a fair and joyful exchange. Sydney unknotted the necklace and slipped the key onto it. She tied the knot again, tightly, and put the necklace back on.

Sydney immediately went to the library, quickly going up the steps and pulling open the tall door. It was just as crowded as the day before. As she walked around she saw people talking and people reading and lounging. She went up to the circulation desk and asked a librarian about the key.

"Is this the key to the room I requested? I requested the key to Ella Abner's room," Sydney said.

"Let me see it please." Ella handed her the key and envelope. "Yes," she said, turning the key over in her hand, "This looks like the key to a room of one's life. Please go to the beginning of the books and a librarian there will direct you to the correct door."

Ella said her thanks and then quickly took off toward the books. Seeing a librarian near the books, she approached her. "Hello, I am looking to get into Ella Abner's room. I have permission and the key right here."

"Yes, I see that," the librarian said, "There are portals all over the library. There is one right here." She led Sydney to a nearby end of a bookshelf and placed Sydney in front of it.

Sydney wondered why she was standing there. Right before her eyes, like the door had appeared on the stump before Ella's eyes, the outline of a door was drawn on the shelf. Then a doorknob and lock appeared and it looked like any door.

In excitement she reached her hand toward the door with the key still around her neck and successfully fit her key into the hole. Turning the key made the necklace too tight and with an impatient sigh she took the key out and took the necklace off. She swiftly entered the key, unlocked the door, and began to open it.

When Sydney opened the door to Ella's life she saw that the room was a continuation of the library, the floor marble and the ceiling tall. There was even a small chandelier. She took a step forward into the room and closed the door behind her. There was the outline of a small circle in the middle of the room. She felt very solitary and did not know what she was doing. She was still gripping the key and loosened her hand around it, putting the necklace back around her neck. Then she steadily walked toward the circle, not knowing what else to do, and stepped inside of it.

It was as though there were a huge vortex, wind rushing at her from every angle. She became dizzy and lightheaded, as though she had not eaten for a long time. She was standing tall, but felt tiny. She saw bits of pictures splashing into her eyes, and heard bits of words screaming into her ears. Her emotions, and she felt a great many different ones, went up and down like the recording of the heart beat on a monitor. Then it all stopped. It had happened very quickly and she knew that she had been filled with knowledge, so much that she did not know what any of it was. She did not know how she would even begin to recognize it.

Sydney had assumed when she was learning about Ella she would actually have to take some effort to ingest the knowledge, but there is was, just like that. Ella's memories and emotions were in Sydney. She looked around the room. It looked just as it had when she first entered. It was silent, although she knew beyond the space were people everywhere.

There was no circular outline around her feet. Natalie walked toward the door leading out and felt like something essential about her had been changed. She knew it had not though. There was just much more that had been added. She now carried herself and Ella and understood this was not to be taken lightly, it was quite a thing to hold.

As Sydney walked, as she put one foot slowly in front of the other, she betrayed no unevenness. She realized though, to carry both yourself and another was challenging. She knew she would need to find a new balance. She knew it would take time to acclimate to this new normal.

That day, that first day, Sydney felt it was too much. She regretted all the new knowledge, she didn't know how to process it. She imagined that she was underwater, drowning. But she learned to carry it, the muscles needed became stronger. She was sore at first, every day, because it was so heavy. As time went on, she carried more than most could have imagined, with ease.

Thirty-three

Time passes differently in the Holding Place. Time

passes to best serve those on Earth. The knowledge Sydney

gained was knowledge she would use from the very beginning,

when Ella had woken up in the field. Had time been

unweighted, been the same in both the Holding Place and on

Earth, these acts would have come too late for Ella.

The Earth's day is measured by the Earth making one

revolution. The Earth's year is measured by the Earth making

its way once around the sun. But in the Holding Place, time is

relative to what a person on Earth needs. Sydney's first month

in the Holding Place passed in minutes on Earth. All the

knowledge she had gained about the best way to help Ella was

in place by the time Ella woke up in the field. All of the

knowledge she had gained about Ella had time to ferment in her

mind and leave behind the brilliant idea of the cove. It was she

who had filled the cove with the binders. It was she who had

put out the apple cider and tomato soup, in mugs she had made

in the potter's studio. She had put out the bread and the wine.

She had put the idea in Marcus's mind to put Ella with the de Angelo's, knowing that Cale was working on her story. She had whispered hopeful things to Ella that became Ella's thoughts. Despite her depression and fall, Ella never broke. She triumphed.

Sydney watched as Ella filled the jar with silver paint. She watched her turn it upside down and coat the inside with silver. She knew what was happening inside Ella's mind and why she was excited. She could also sense Ella's emotions. She understood Ella had been carrying around chaos that she was now ready to let go of. She watched Ella turn the jar upside down, watched the silver coat it. It somehow made Sydney nervous, as if the paint would burst through the lid, marking the ground. This though, exactly this, was what Ella intended. Sydney watched the next night, when Ella stood near the telephone pole. She watched Ella lift the jar with both hands, above her head and reaching behind her back. The then forcefully brought it back over her head, gathering speed. When it was right above her head she let it go, and it crashed into the pole, the jar breaking and the paint splattering. Mostly it splattered onto the pole, but also on the street below. Ella smiled, her eyes boring into the spatter. Sydney knew this was good. She was letting go of the chaos and all that had gone with it, she was freeing herself.

In the beginning of things Sydney sometimes felt sad or sympathy for Ella. In the beginning of her memories with Corey, she felt that Ella was at serious risk of breaking, and the pain Ella felt was hard to watch. Sydney understood this was not a productive or sustainable stance to take. Ella did not need anybody to stretch out these feelings, to feel sorry for her beyond an initial reaction. Sydney saw Ella as her counterpart, an equal. Stretching out the feelings of sympathy for Ella seemed to make them unequal. But truly, Sydney learned what all people in the Holding Place come to understand – no matter how we look on the outside, what our pain or dysfunction, what our riches or poverty, in our deepest cores, in our organic souls – no one is better or worse than their neighbor.

Epilogue: Somer

We all have the capability to shift and slide to different corners of ourselves. Ella and I both lost our memory when we were merged into one person. We became different aspects of the same personality and we would shift and slide based on what happened. When we read the binders, we were Ella, for that had been her life. When we were with Natalie and it felt familiar, we were me, Somer, her biological sister.

When faced with experiences, be it hardships or joys, different parts of us are brought to the surface. People sometimes realize an aspect of their personality they did not know was there. With us, this tendency was even more complex.

From the moment we were splintered we became different people. Ella and I were one, but grew up with different experiences. The hardships Ella faced shaped her as much as the ease I faced. The differences we experienced were constant and great. We, though one soul, were more like sisters. When we were first splintered it was as though we both had lost sight in one eye. We each could still see but there was an awareness we each did not have. Despite the splintering we were both whole and lived genuine lives before we were joined on Earth.

It's not an absolute, not as though what Ella experienced early on was all bad, and what I experienced was all good. We both had our unique joys and sorrows. We both had stagnations and undertakings in our lives. When we were joined it was not as though I was trapped inside Ella. We had simply gone back to the way things were in the beginning. The tragedy of my death in the beginning, a person who was new to the world, an infant, did not negate the fact I would grow up with a fully formed self. The miracle of Ella did not negate the fact that her soul was already my soul.

There is only so much a person can carry. My memory, while on Earth, would never fully come back. It was Ella's body we had been merged into. The binders were her life. The world was her life. The parents were her parents. The people were her people. At first, we only had the ability to be Ella. To have my memories wrapped into us as well would not have fit. The flashes of familiarity we felt started with Natalie. It would take years for us to gain the inexpressible identity of Somer. It was never possible for us to say, 'there is this other whole other part of me here.' It grew to the point, though, that we knew.

Like Ella, like we, discovered, we could hold her life only because it was padded to her bones, we came to discover that was the only way we could hold me too. When the day came that we had both Ella's memories and a complete awareness of me, we seemed to be at capacity. Still though, there was room for more. We had room for what would come with the future. It seems that the fuller of life we are, the more it compacts and concentrates, and makes room for more.

There was a time in the beginning when we knew on a deep level that we were both Ella and Somer. We could not have put it into words, but we knew there was a distinct edge to us. We knew that who we were fell into a unique category. There was a sense that we were different.

It happened the night we went to the telephone pole with the jar of paint. That night we took our frustrations, worry, and confusion, and symbolically let them go. We chose not to deal with them, not to process them, just to let them go. They had filled up the past and shaded the future, and we no longer saw a need for them. We took the jar and smashed it into the telephone pole. The jar had broken and the paint had splattered.

The moment of awareness was when we bent down, picking up the glass from the road. As we scraped the shards of glass from the road with Ella's fingers, Ella began to bleed. When we looked at the blood on her fingers, we believed it was intimately Ella's and not at all hers. As we swept the glass with her fingers, the blood and paint mixed together. They seemed to come together without anything to separate them. We sensed how we walked intimately with one another, and how we carried one another. We were one element, transformed into something new when put together.

Ella would never have the same grief I once had, longing to be on Earth. It was I who had so much fight in her when she was born. I was who Henry, the man for who the Holding Place was his Final Place, sensed needed to be in the world. But we all need to be in the world, this is what I learned being taken away from it, there is a purpose for everyone on Earth. Sometimes life is cut short and that is an inevitability of some human lives. There is another life, of course, waiting for us but it is Earth that is a wonderful privilege. Once you have died the chance for that life is gone. It was truly a miracle that my soul remained in the world.

Like every person alive, our soul shaped Earth. The world would not have been the same had our soul not been in it. That is what I want to tell you, at the conclusion of this story. Not all souls make it to birth, and not all souls survive a full lifetime after birth. The Earth is malleable. What we do makes a difference. Your soul is here to play with the world. Interact with it and be immersed in it. Like Ella's birth was a miracle, we are all miracles. Nobody more or less so than anybody else.

It was a miracle I grew up in The Holding Place and was joined with Ella at the age of twenty. When we died, many years later, our soul was divided again. We were intimate friends and sisters in the Holding Place, living next to each other. We were surrounded by different expanded families. I was satisfied to have experienced life on Earth.

My soul had fought to be in the world, not unlike the many other souls that have fought and lost. Because of Henry I was given the privilege of living on Earth. When we first got back to the Holding Place, when we died at 89, I went to Henry and told him of our journey.

"I could not fully remember what happened before the field, until now." I told him, "Now I believe I was always meant to take this journey."

"You were, my child," he said. Thank you for fighting for life, you have been my favorite miracle.

I smiled at him, and thought of Ella. It had not been meant for this to happen. It had only been because of Henry's miracle.

Even the pain we felt was beautiful. Most of all, it was authentic. We lived on Earth. We were both of us, we shared a soul. We experienced love and pain. We were human.

When we went to the Holding Place, my task was different than it had been. It was no longer to spread joy. My task was to help those who died at or near birth transition to the Holding Place. To provide a home for them until they were fully integrated into life in the Holding Place with an expanded family. It was as though all the joy I had spread before had been collected and given to me again. I saw souls in the beginning, in their most fragile and vulnerable state. I saw souls who would not live on Earth. They would not be lucky in the way I had been lucky. They would grow up in the Holding Place. They would be enveloped in love. They would never be hurt. That is pretty lucky too.

A note from Caroline

Dear Readers,

Thank you for reading my book, a story hosting deep truths of my own life, and deep longings I have for the world we live in. It is full of so much that brings pain and joy. The Holding Place is based on no specific religion, but more a conglomeration of my idea of a comforting, hopeful, purposeful, and healing place. I don't see it as a utopia because people still have hardships. If there were no hardships, though, it would be much harder to relate to the world in a real way. So many people break in our world, this Earth, and I like to imagine a place absent from too much hardship, a place where we can rest in comfort and care for as long as we need.

Nobody will relate to every part of this story. But I hope that you will find yourself somewhere, in some sentence, and that you will trust that all humans are DNA milliseconds off each other.

Truly to write this book, each person I have known has impacted who I have become and the stories I write. Some have been extraordinary influences on my life. I thank you profusely.

Caroline
2017

Printed in Great Britain
by Amazon

18653443R00202